*

CLORINDA WALKS IN HEAVEN

Tales

CAN SUCH THINGS BE? by Ambrose Bierce
THE BLACK DOG by A. E. Coppard
THE AUTOBIOGRAPHY OF A SUPER-TRAMP by W. H. Davies
BABBITT by Sinclair Lewis
THE CRAFT OF FICTION by Percy Lubbock
EARLHAM by Percy Lubbock
WIDE SEAS AND MANY LANDS by Arthur Mason
SELECTED PREJUDICES by H. L. Mencken
THE MIND IN THE MAKING by James Harvey Robinson
THE WAY OF ALL FLESH by Samuel Butler
EREWHON by Samuel Butler
EREWHON REVISITED by Samuel Butler
ADAM AND EVE AND PINCH ME by A. E. Coppard
DUBLINERS by James Joyce
DOG AND DUCK by Arthur Machen
KAI LUNG'S GOLDEN HOURS by Ernest Bramah
ANGELS AND MINISTERS by Laurence Housman
THE WALLET OF KAI LUNG by Ernest Bramah
TWILIGHT IN ITALY by D. H. Lawrence
THE DREAM by H. G. Wells
ROMAN PICTURES by Percy Lubbock

Uniform with this volume

CLORINDA
WALKS IN HEAVEN

Tales by
A. E. COPPARD

LONDON
JONATHAN CAPE 30 BEDFORD SQUARE

FIRST PUBLISHED IN 1922
FIRST ISSUED IN THE TRAVELLERS' LIBRARY 1926

Printed in Guernsey by the Star and Gazette Co., Ltd.

TO MRS. FLYNN

CONTENTS

	PAGE
THE HURLY-BURLY	15
CLORINDA WALKS IN HEAVEN	35
THE CHERRY TREE	47
THE ELIXIR OF YOUTH	57
FELIX TINCLER	77
CRAVEN ARMS	99
A BROADSHEET BALLAD	157
COTTON	173
POMONA'S BABE	193

THE HURLY-BURLY

CHAPTER ONE

The Hurly-Burly

*

THE Weetmans – mother, son, and daughter – lived on a thriving farm. It was small enough, God knows; but it had always been a turbulent place of abode. For the servant it was 'Phemy, do this,' or 'Phemy, have you done that?' from dawn to dark, and even from dark to dawn there was a hovering of unrest. The widow Weetman, a partial invalid, was the only figure that manifested any semblance of tranquillity; and it was a misleading one, for she sat day after day on her large hams, knitting and nodding, and lifting her grey face only to grumble, her spectacled eyes transfixing the culprit with a basilisk glare. And her daughter Alice, the housekeeper, who had a large face, a dominating face, in some respects she was all face, was like a blast in a corridor with her 'Maize for the hens, Phemy! – More firewood, Phemy! – Who has set the trap in the harness room? – Come along! – Have you scoured the skimming pans? – Why not? – Where are you idling? – Come along Phemy, I have no time to waste this morning; you really must help me!' It was not only in the house that this cataract of industry flowed; outside there was activity enough for a regiment. A master-farmer's work consists largely of a series of conversations with other master-farmers, a long-winded way of doing long-headed things; but Glastonbury Weetman, the son, was not like that at all; he was the incarnation of energy, always doing and doing, chock-full of orders, adjurations, objurgations, blame, and blasphemy. That was the kind of place Phemy Madigan worked at. No one could rest on laurels there. The farm and the home possessed everybody, lock, stock, and barrel; work was like a tiger, it ate you up implacably. The Weetmans did not mind – they liked being eaten by such a tiger.

After six or seven years of this Alice went back to marry an old sweetheart in Canada, where the Weetmans had originally come from; but Phemy's burden was in no way lessened thereby. There were as many things to wash and sew and darn; there was always a cart of churns about to dash for a train it could not possibly catch, or a horse to shoe that could not possibly be spared. Weetman hated to see his people merely walking. 'Run over to the barn for that hayfork!' or 'Slip across to the ricks, quick, now!' he would cry; and if ever an unwary hen hampered his path it only did so once – and no more. His labourers were mere things of flesh and blood, but they occasionally resented his ceaseless flagellations. Glas Weetman did not like to be impeded or controverted; one day in a rage he had smashed that lumbering loon of a carter called Gathercole. For this he was sent to gaol for a month.

The day after he had been sentenced Phemy Madigan, alone in the house with Mrs. Weetman, had waked at the usual early hour. It was a foggy September morning; Sampson and his boy Daniel were clattering pails in the dairy shed. The girl felt sick and gloomy as she dressed; it was a wretched house to work in, crickets in the kitchen, cockroaches in the garret, spiders and mice everywhere. It was an old, long, low house; she knew that when she descended the stairs the walls would be stained with autumnal dampness, the banisters and rails oozing with moisture. She wished she was a lady and married, and living in a palace fifteen stories high.

It was fortunate that she was big and strong, though she had only been a charity girl taken from the workhouse by the Weetmans when she was fourteen years old. That was seven years ago. It was fortunate that she was well fed at the farm, very well indeed; it was the one virtue of the place. But her meals did not counterbalance things; that farm ate up the body and blood of people. And at times the pressure was charged with a special excitation, as if a taut elastic thong had been plucked and released with a reverberating ping.

It was so on this morning. Mrs. Weetman was dead in her bed.

At that crisis a new sense descended upon the girl, a sense of responsibility. She was not in fear, she felt no grief or surprise. It concerned her in some way, but she herself was unconcerned, and she slid without effort into the position of mistress of the farm. She opened a window and looked out of doors. A little way off a boy with a red scarf stood by an open gate.

'Oi – oi, kup, kup, kup!' he cried to the cows

in that field. Some of the cows, having got up, stared amiably at him, others sat on, ignoring his hail, while one or two plodded deliberately towards him. 'Oi – oi, kup, kup, kup!'

'Lazy rascal, that boy,' remarked Phemy; 'we shall have to get rid of him. Dan'l! Come here, Dan'l!' she screamed, waving her arm wildly. 'Quick!'

She sent him away for police and doctor. At the inquest there were no relatives in England who could be called upon, no other witnesses than Phemy. After the funeral she wrote a letter to Glastonbury Weetman in gaol, informing him of his bereavement, but to this he made no reply. Meanwhile the work of the farm was pressed forward under her control; for though she was revelling in her personal release from the torment, she would not permit others to share her intermission. She had got Mrs. Weetman's keys and her box of money. She paid the two men and the boy their wages week by week. The last of the barley was reaped, the oats stacked, the roots hoed, the churns sent daily under her supervision. And always she was bustling the men.

'O dear me, these lazy rogues!' she would complain to the empty room. 'They waste time, so it's robbery – it *is* robbery. You may wear yourself to the bone, and what does it signify to such as them? All the responsibility too! They would take your skin if they could get it off you – and they can't!'

She kept such a sharp eye on the corn and meal and eggs that Sampson grew surly. She placated him by handing him Mr. Weetman's gun and a few cartridges, saying: 'Just shoot me a couple of rabbits over in the warren when you get time.' At the end of the day Mr. Sampson had not succeeded in killing a rabbit, so he kept the gun and the cartridges many more days. Phemy was really happy. The gloom of the farm had disappeared. The farm and everything about it looked beautiful, beautiful indeed with its yard full of ricks, the pond full of ducks, the fields full of sheep and cattle, and the trees still full of leaves and birds. She flung maize about the yard; the hens scampered towards it and the young pigs galloped, quarrelling over the grains which they groped and snuffled for, grinding each one separately in their iron jaws,

20

while the white pullets stalked delicately among
them, picked up the maize seeds – one, two,
three – and swallowed them like ladies. Sometimes on cold mornings she would go outside
and give an apple to the fat bay pony when he
galloped back from the station. He would stand
puffing with a kind of rapture, the wind from
his nostrils discharging in the frosty air vague
shapes like smoky trumpets. Presently, upon his
hide, a little ball of liquid mysteriously suspired,
grew, slid, dropped from his flanks into the
road. And then drops would begin to come
from all parts of him until the road beneath was
dabbled by a shower from his dew-distilling outline. Phemy would say:

'The wretches! They were so late they drove
him near distracted, poor thing. Lazy rogues,
but wait till master comes back, they'd better be
careful!'

And if any friendly person in the village asked
her, 'How are you getting on up there, Phemy?'
she would reply, 'Oh, as well as you can expect
with so much to be done – and such men!' The
interlocutor might hint that there was no occasion in the circumstances to distress oneself, but

then Phemy would be vexed. To her, honesty was as holy as the Sabbath to a little child. Behind her back they jested about her foolishness; but after all, wisdom isn't a process, it's a result, it's the fruit of the tree. One can't be wise, one can only be fortunate.

On the last day of her elysium the workhouse master and the chaplain had stalked over the farm, shooting partridges. In the afternoon she met them and asked for a couple of birds for Weetman's return on the morrow. The workhouse was not far away, it was on a hill facing west, and at sunset-time its windows would often catch the glare so powerfully that the whole building seemed to burn like a box of contained and smokeless fire. Very beautiful it looked to Phemy.

2

The men had come to work punctually, and Phemy herself found so much to do that she had no time to give the pony an apple. She cleared the kitchen once and for all of the pails, guns, harness, and implements that so hampered its domestic intention, and there were abundant signs elsewhere of a new impulse at work in the establishment. She did not know at what hour to expect the prisoner, so she often went to the garden-gate and glanced up the road. The night had been wild with windy rain, but morn was sparkling clear, though breezy still. Crisp leaves rustled along the road where the polished chestnuts beside the parted husks lay in numbers, mixed with coral buds of the yews. The sycamore leaves were black rags, but the delicate elm foliage fluttered down like yellow stars. There was a brown field neatly adorned with white coned heaps of turnips, behind it a small upland of deeply green lucerne, behind that nothing but blue sky and rolling cloud. The turnips, washed by the rain, were creamy polished globes.

When at last he appeared she scarcely knew him. Glas Weetman was a big, though not fleshy, man of thirty, with a large boyish face and a flat bald head. Now he had a thick dark beard. He was hungry, but his first desire was to be shaved. He stood before the kitchen mirror, first clipping the beard away with scissors, and as he lathered the remainder he said:

23

'Well, it's a bad state of things, this – my sister dead and my mother gone to America. What shall us do?'

He perceived in the glass that she was smiling.

'There's naught funny in it, my comic gal!' he bawled indigantly. 'What are you laughing at?'

'I weren't laughing. It's your mother that's dead.'

'My mother that's dead, I know.'

'And Miss Alice that's gone to America.'

'To America, I know, I know, so you can stop making your bullock's eyes and get me something to eat. What's been going on here?'

She gave him an outline of affairs. He looked at her sternly when he asked her about his sweetheart.

'Has Rosa Beauchamp been along here?'

'No,' said Phemy, and he was silent. She was surprised at the question. The Beauchamps were such respectable high-up people that to Phemy's simple mind they could not possibly favour an alliance now with a man that had been in prison; it was absurd, but she did not say so to him. And she was bewildered to find that her conviction was wrong, for Rosa came along later in the day and everything between her master and his sweetheart was just as before; Phemy had not divined so much love and forgiveness in high-up people.

It was the same with everything else. The old harsh rushing life was resumed, Weetman turned to his farm with an accelerated vigour to make up for lost time, and the girl's golden week or two of ease became an unforgotten dream. The pails, the guns, the harness crept back into the kitchen. Spiders, cockroaches and mice were more noticeable than ever before, and Weetman himself seemed embittered, harsher. Time alone could never still him, there was a force in his frame, a buzzing in his blood. But there was a difference between them now; Phemy no longer feared him. She obeyed him, it is true, with eagerness, she worked in the house like a woman and in the fields like a man. They ate their meals together, and from this dissonant comradeship the girl, in a dumb kind of way, began to love him.

One April evening, on coming in from the fields, he found her lying on the couch beneath the window, dead plumb fast asleep, with no meal ready at all. He flung his bundle of harness to the flags and bawled angrily to her. To his surprise she did not stir. He was somewhat abashed; he stepped over to look at her. She was lying on her side. There was a large rent in her bodice between sleeve and shoulder; her flesh looked soft and agreeable to him. Her shoes had slipped off to the floor; her lips were folded in a pout.

'Why, she's quite a pretty cob,' he murmured. 'She's all right, she's just tired, the Lord above knows what for.'

But he could not rouse the sluggard. Then a fancy moved him to lift her in his arms; he carried her from the kitchen and, staggering up the stairs, laid the sleeping girl on her own bed. He then went downstairs and ate pie and drank beer in the candlelight, guffawing once or twice: 'A pretty cob, rather.' As he stretched himself after the meal a new notion amused him: he put a plateful of food upon a tray, together with a mug of beer and the candle. Doffing his heavy

26

boots and leggings, he carried the tray into Phemy's room. And he stopped there.

3

The new circumstance that thus slipped into her life did not effect any noticeable alteration of its general contour and progress. Weetman did not change towards her. Phemy accepted his mastership not alone because she loved him, but because her powerful sense of loyalty covered all the possible opprobrium. She did not seem to mind his continued relations with Rosa.

Towards midsummer one evening Glastonbury came in in the late dusk. Phemy was there in the darkened kitchen. 'Master!' she said immediately he entered. He stopped before her. She continued: 'Something's happened.'

'Huh, while the world goes popping round something shall always happen!'

'It's me — I'm took — a baby, master,' she said. He stood stock-still. His back was to the light, she could not see the expression on his face, perhaps he wanted to embrace her.

'Let's have a light, sharp,' he said in his

27

brusque way. 'The supper smells good, but I can't see what I'm smelling, and I can only fancy what I be looking at.'

She lit the candles and they ate supper in silence. Afterwards he sat away from the table with his legs outstretched and crossed, hands sunk into pockets, pondering while the girl cleared the table. Soon he put his powerful arm around her waist and drew her to sit on his knees.

'Are ye sure o' that?' he demanded.

She was sure.

'Quite?'

She was quite sure.

'Ah, well then,' he sighed conclusively, 'we'll be married!'

The girl sprang to her feet. 'No, no, no! How can you be married? You don't mean that — not married — there's Miss Beauchamp!' She paused and added a little unsteadily, 'She's your true love, master.'

'Ay! but I'll not wed her!' he cried sternly. 'If there's no gainsaying this that's come on you I'll stand to my guns. It's right and proper for we to have a marriage.'

28

His great thick-fingered hands rested upon his knees; the candles threw a wash of light upon his polished leggings; he stared in the fireless grate.

'But we do not want to do that,' said the girl dully and doubtfully. 'You have given your ring to her, you've given her your word. I don't want you to do this for me. It's all right, master, it's all right.'

'Are ye daft?' he cried. 'I tell you we'll wed. Don't keep clacking about Rosa – I'll stand to my guns.' He paused before adding, 'She'd gimme the rightabout, fine now – don't you see, stupid? – but I'll not give her the chance.'

Her eyes were lowered. 'She's your true love, master.'

'What would become of you and your child? Ye couldn't bide here!'

'No,' said the trembling girl.

'I'm telling you what we must do, modest and proper; there's naught else to be done, and I'm middling glad of it, I am. Life's a see-saw affair. I'm middling glad of this.'

So, soon, without a warning to anyone, least of all to Rosa Beauchamp, they were married by

the registrar. The change in her domestic status
produced no other change; in marrying Weetman she but married all his ardour, she was
swept into its current. She helped to milk cows,
she boiled nauseating messes for pigs, chopped
mangolds, mixed meal, and sometimes drove a
harrow in his windy fields. Though they slept
together, she was still his servant. Sometimes he
called her his 'pretty little cob,' and then she
knew he was fond of her. But in general his
custom was disillusioning. His way with her was
his way with his beasts; he knew what he
wanted, it was easy to get. If for a brief space a
little romantic flower began to bud in her breast
it was frozen as a bud, and the vague longing
disappeared at length from her eyes. And she
became aware that Rosa Beauchamp was not yet
done with; somewhere in the darkness of the
fields Glastonbury still met her. Phemy did not
mind.

In the new year she bore him a son that died
as it came to life. Glas was angry at that, as
angry as if he had lost a horse. He felt that he
had been duped, that the marriage had been a
stupid sacrifice, and in this he was savagely sup-

ported by Rosa. And yet Phemy did not mind;
the farm had got its grip upon her, it was consuming her body and blood.

Weetman was just going to drive into town;
he sat fuming in the trap behind the fat bay
pony.

'Bring me that whip from the passage!' he
shouted. 'There's never a dam thing handy!'

Phemy appeared with the whip. 'Take me
with you,' she said.

'God-a-mighty! What for? I be comen back
in an hour. They ducks want looking over, and
you've all the taties to grade.'

She stared at him irresolutely.

'And who's to look after the house? You
know it won't lock up – the key's lost. Get up
there!'

He cracked his whip in the air as the pony
dashed away.

In the summer Phemy fell sick, her arm
swelled enormously. The doctor came again and
again. It was blood-poisoning, caught from a
diseased cow that she had milked with a cut
finger. A nurse arrived, but Phemy knew she
was doomed, and though tortured with pain she

was for once vexed and protestant. For it was a
June night, soft and nubile, with a marvellous
moon; a nightingale threw its impetuous garland
into the air. She lay listening to it and thinking
with sad pleasure of the time when Glastonbury
was in prison, how grand she was in her solitude,
ordering everything for the best and working
superbly. She wanted to go on and on for evermore, though she knew she had never known
peace in maidenhood or marriage. The troubled
waters of the world never ceased to flow; in the
night there was no rest—only darkness. Nothing
could emerge now. She was leaving it all to
Rosa Beauchamp. Glastonbury was gone out
somewhere—perhaps to meet Rosa in the fields.
There was the nightingale, and it was very
bright outside.

'Nurse,' moaned the dying girl, 'what was I
born into the world at all for?'

CLORINDA WALKS IN HEAVEN

C

Clorinda Walks in Heaven

*

Miss Sarth, Clorinda Smith, desired not to die on a wet day. Her speculations on the possibilities of one's demise were quite ingenuous and had their mirth, but she shrank from that figure of her dim little soul – and it was only dimly that she could figure it at all – approaching the pathways of the Boundless in a damp, bedraggled condition.

'But the rain couldn't harm your spirit,' declared her comforting friends.

'Why not?' asked Clorinda. 'If there is a ghost of me, why not a ghost of the rain?'

There were other aspects, delectable and illusive, of this imagined apotheosis, but Clorinda always hoped – against hope be it said – that it wouldn't be wet. On three evenings there had been a bow in the sky, and on the day she died rain poured in fury. With a golden key she unlocked the life out of her bosom and moved away without fear, as if a great light had sprung suddenly under her feet in a little dark place,

CHAPTER TWO

Clorinda Walks in Heaven

*

Miss Smith, Clorinda Smith, desired not to die on a wet day. Her speculations on the possibilities of one's demise were quite ingenuous and had their mirth, but she shrunk from that figure of her dim little soul – and it was only dimly that she could figure it at all – approaching the pathways of the Boundless in a damp, bedraggled condition.

'But the rain couldn't harm your spirit,' declared her comforting friends.

'Why not?" asked Clorinda. 'If there is a ghost of me, why not a ghost of the rain?'

There were other aspects, delectable and illusive, of this imagined apotheosis, but Clorinda always hoped – against hope be it said – that it wouldn't be wet. On three evenings there had been a bow in the sky, and on the day she died rain poured in fury. With a golden key she unlocked the life out of her bosom and moved away without fear, as if a great light had sprung suddenly under her feet in a little dark place, into a region where things became starkly real and one seemed to live like the beams rolling on the tasselled corn in windy acres. There was calmness in those translucent leagues and the undulation amid a vast implacable light until she drifted, like a feather fallen from an un-guessed star, into a place which was extraordin-arily like the noon-day world, so green and warm was its valley.

A little combe lay between some low hills of turf, and on a green bank beside a few large rocks was a man mending a ladder of white new-shaven willow studded with large brass nails, mending it with hard knocks that sounded clearly. The horizon was terraced only just be-yond and above him, for the hills rolled steeply up. Thin pads of wool hung in the arch of the ultimate heavens, but towards the end of the valley the horizon was clouded with clouds torn and disbattled. Two cows, a cow of white and a cow of tan, squatted where one low hill held up, as it were, the sunken limits of the sky. There were larks – in such places the lark sings for ever – and thrushes – the wind vaguely active – seven white ducks – a farm. Each nook

36

was a flounce of blooms and a bower for birds. Passing close to the man — he was sad and pre-occupied, dressed in a little blue tunic — she touched his arm as if to inquire a direction, saying 'Jacob!'

She did not know what she would have asked of him, but he gave her no heed and she again called to him: 'Jacob!' He did not seem even to see her, so she went to the large white gates at the end of the valley and approached a railway crossing. She had to wait a long time, for trains of a vastness and grandeur were passing without sound. Strange advertisements on the hoardings and curious direction posts gathered some of her attention. She observed that in every possible situation, on any available post or stone, people had carved initials, sometimes a whole name, often with a date, and Clorinda experienced a doubt of the genuineness of some of these, so remote was the antiquity implied. At last the trains were all gone by, and as the barriers swung back she crossed the permanent way.

There was neither ambiguity in her movements nor surprise in her apprehensions. She just crossed over to a group of twenty or thirty

37

men who moved to welcome her. They were barelegged, sandal-footed, lightly clad in beautiful loose tunics of peacock and cinnamon, which bore not so much the significance of colour as the quality of light. One of them rushed eagerly forward, crying 'Clorinda!' offering to her a long coloured scarf. Strangely, as he came closer, he grew less perceivable; Clorinda was aware in a flash that she was viewing him by some other mechanism than that of her two eyes. In a moment he utterly disappeared and she felt herself rapt into his being, caressed with faint caresses, and troubled with dim faded ecstasies and recognitions not wholly agreeable. The other men stood grouped around them, glancing with half-closed cynical eyes. Those who stood farthest away were more clearly seen: in contiguity a presence could only be divined, resting only – but how admirably! – in the nurture of one's mind.

'What is it?' Clorinda asked: and all the voices replied, 'Yes, we know you!'

She felt herself released, and the figure of the man rejoined the waiting group. 'I was your husband Reuben,' said the first man slowly, and

Clorinda, who had been a virgin throughout her short life, exclaimed 'Yes, yes, dear Reuben!' with momentary tremors and a queer fugitive drift of doubt. She stood there, a spook of comprehending being, and all the uncharted reefs in the map of her mind were anxiously engaging her. For a time she was absorbed by this new knowledge.

Then another voice spoke:

'I was your husband Raphael!'

'I know, I know,' said Clorinda, turning to the speaker, 'we lived in Judæa.'

'And we dwelt in the valley of the Nile,' said another, 'in the years that are gone.'

'And I too . . . and I too . . . and I too,' they all clamoured, turning angrily upon themselves.

Clorinda pulled the strange scarf from her shoulders where Reuben had left it, and, handling it so, she became aware of her many fugitive sojournings upon the earth. It seemed that all of her past had become knit in the scarf into a compact pattern of beauty and ugliness of which she was entirely aware, all its multiplexity being immediately resolved . . . the habitations

39

with cave men, and the lesser human unit of the lesser later day, Patagonian, Indian, Cossack, Polynesian, Jew . . . of such stuff the pattern was intimately woven, and there were little plangent perfect moments of the past that fell into order in the web. Clorinda watching the great seabird with pink feet louting above the billows that roared upon Iceland, or Clorinda hanging her girdle upon the ebony hooks of the image of Tanteelee. She had taken voyaging drafts upon the whole world, cataract, jungle and desert, ingle and pool and strand, ringing the changes upon a whole gamut of masculine endeavour . . . from a prophet to a haberdasher. She could feel each little life hung now as in a sarsnet of cameos upon her visible breasts: thereby for these . . . these *men* . . . she was draped in an eternal wonder. But she could not recall any image of her past life in *these* realms, save only that her scarf was given back to her on every return by a man of these men.

She could remember with humility her transient passions for them all. None, not one, had ever given her the measure of her own desire, a strong harsh flame that fashioned and tempered its own body; nothing but a nebulous glow that was riven into embers before its beam had sweetened into pride. She had gone from them childless always and much as a little child.

From the crowd of quarrelling ghosts a new figure detached itself, and in its approach it subdued that vague vanishing which had been so perplexing to Clorinda. Out of the crowd it slipped, and loomed lovingly beside her, took up her thought and the interrogation that came into her mind.

'No,' it said gravely, 'there is none greater than these. The ultimate reaches of man's mind produce nothing but images of men.'

'But,' said Clorinda, 'do you mean that our ideals, previsions of a vita-nuova. . . .'

'Just so,' it continued, 'a mere intoxication. Even here you cannot escape the singular dower of dreams . . . you can be drunk with dreams more easily and more permanently than with drugs.'

The group of husbands had ceased their quarrelling to listen; Clorinda swept them with her glances thoughtfully and doubtfully.

'Could mankind be so poor,' the angel resumed, 'as poor as these, if it housed something greater than itself?'

With a groan the group of outworn husbands drew away. Clorinda turned to her companion with disappointment and some dismay . . .'I hardly understand yet . . . is this all then, just. . . .'

'Yes,' it replied, 'just the ghost of the world.'

She turned unhappily and looked back across the gateway into the fair combe with its cattle, its fine grass, and the man working diligently therein. A sense of bleak loneliness began to possess her; here, then, was no difference save that there were no correlations, no consequences; nothing had any effect except to produce the ghost of a ghost. There was already in the hinterland of her apprehensions a ghost of her new ghostship: she was to be followed by herself, pursued by figures of her own ceaseless being!

She looked at the one by her side: 'Who are you?' she asked, and at the question the group of men drew again very close to them.

'I am your unrealised desires,' it said: 'Did

you think that the dignity of virginhood, rarely and deliberately chosen, could be so brief and barren? Why, that pure idea was my own immaculate birth, and I was born, the living mate of you.'

The hungry-eyed men shouted with laughter.

'Go away!' screamed Clorinda to them; 'I do not want you.'

Although they went she could hear the echoes of their sneering as she took the arm of her new lover. 'Let us go,' she said, pointing to the man in the combe, 'and speak to him.' As they approached the man he lifted his ladder hugely in the air and dashed it to the ground so passionately that it broke.

'Angry man! angry man!' mocked Clorinda. He turned towards her fiercely. Clorinda began to fear him; the muscles and knots of his limbs were uncouth like the gnarl of old trees; she made a little pretence of no more observing him.

'Now what is it like,' said she jocularly to the angel at her side, and speaking of her old home, 'what is it like now at Weston-super-Mare?'

At that foolish question the man with the

ladder reached forth an ugly hand and twitched
the scarf from her shoulders.

It cannot now be told to what remoteness she
had come, or on what roads her undirected feet
had travelled there, but certain it is that in that
moment she was gone. . . . Why, where or
how cannot be established: whether she was
swung in a blast of annihilation into the utter-
most gulfs, or withdrawn for her beauty into
that mysterious Nox; into some passionate com-
munion with the eternal husbands, or into some
eternal combat with their passionate other wives
. . . from our scrutiny at least she passed for
ever.

It is true there was a beautiful woman of this
name who lay for a month in a deep trance in
the West of England. On her recovery she was
balladed about in the newspapers and upon the
halls for quite a time, and indeed her notoriety
brought requests for her autograph from all parts
of the world, and an offer of marriage from a
Quaker potato merchant. But she tenderly re-
fused him and became one of those faded grey
old maids who wear their virginity like anti-
quated armour.

44

THE CHERRY TREE

The Cherry Tree

*

THERE was uproar somewhere among the back-yards of Australia Street. It was so alarming that people at their midday meal sat still and stared at one another. A fortnight before murder had been done in the street, in broad daylight, with a chopper; people were nervous. An upper window was thrown open and a startled and startling head exposed.

'It's that young devil, Johnny Flynn, again! Killing rats!' shouted Mrs. Knatchbole, shaking her fist towards the Flynns' backyard. Mrs. Knatchbole was ugly; she had a goitred neck and a sharp skinny nose with an orb shining at its end, constant as grief.

'You wait, my boy, till your mother comes home, you just wait!' invited this apparition, but Johnny was gazing sickly at the body of a big rat slaughtered by the dogs of his friend George. The uproar was caused by the quarrelling of the dogs, possibly for honours, but more probably, as is the custom of victors, for loot.

CHAPTER THREE

The Cherry Tree

*

THERE was uproar somewhere among the back-yards of Australia Street. It was so alarming that people at their midday meal sat still and stared at one another. A fortnight before murder had been done in the street, in broad daylight, with a chopper; people were nervous. An upper window was thrown open and a startled and startling head exposed.

'It's that young devil, Johnny Flynn, again! Killing rats!' shouted Mrs. Knatchbole, shaking her fist towards the Flynns' backyard. Mrs. Knatchbole was ugly; she had a goitred neck and a sharp skinny nose with an orb shining at its end, constant as grief.

'You wait, my boy, till your mother comes home, you just wait!' invited this apparition, but Johnny was gazing sickly at the body of a big rat slaughtered by the dogs of his friend George. The uproar was caused by the quarrelling of the dogs, possibly for honours, but more probably, as is the custom of victors, for loot.

'Bob down!' warned George, but Johnny bobbed up to catch the full anger of those baleful Knatchbole eyes. The urchin put his fingers promptly to his nose.

'Look at that for eight years old,' screamed the lady. 'Eight years old 'e is! As true as God's my maker I'll . . .'

The impending vow was stayed and blasted for ever, Mrs. Knatchbole being taken with a fit of sneezing, whereupon the boys uttered some derisive 'Haw-haws!'

So Mrs. Knatchbole met Mrs. Flynn that night as she came from work, Mrs. Flynn being a widow who toiled daily and dreadfully at a laundry and perforce left her children, except for their school hours, to their own devices. The encounter was an emphatic one and the tired widow promised to admonish her boy.

'But it's all right, Mrs. Knatchbole, he's going from me in a week, to his uncle in London he is going, a person of wealth, and he'll be no annoyance to ye then. I'm ashamed that he misbehaves but he's no bad boy really.'

At home his mother's remonstrances reduced Johnny to repentance and silence; he felt base

48

indeed; he wanted to do something great and worthy at once to offset it all; he wished he had got some money, he'd have gone and bought her a bottle of stout – he knew she liked stout.

'Why do ye vex people so, Johnny?' asked Mrs. Flynn wearily. 'I work my fingers to the bone for ye, week in and week out. Why can't ye behave like Pomony?'

His sister was a year younger than him; her name was Mona, which Johnny's elegant mind had disliked. One day he re-baptised her; Pomona she became and Pomona she remained. The Flynns sat down to supper. 'Never mind about all that, mum,' said the boy, kissing her as he passed her chair, 'talk to us about the cherry tree!' The cherry tree, luxuriantly blooming, was the crown of the mother's memories of her youth and her father's farm; around the myth of its wonderful blossoms and fruit she could weave garlands of romance, and to her own mind, as well as to the minds of her children, it became a heavenly symbol of her old lost home, grand with acres and delightful with orchard and full pantry. What wonder that in her humorous narration the joys were multiplied and magnified until even Johnny was obliged to intervene. 'Look here, how many horses did your father have, mum . . . really, though?' Mrs. Flynn became vague, cast a furtive glance at this son of hers and then gulped with laughter until she recovered her ground with; 'Ah, but there *was* a cherry tree!' It was a grand supper – actually a polony and some potatoes. Johnny knew this was because he was going away. Ever since it was known that he was to go to London they had been having something special like this, or sheep's trotters, or a pig's tail. Mother seemed to grow kinder and kinder to him. He wished he had some money, he would like to buy her a bottle of stout – he knew she liked stout.

Well, Johnny went away to live with his uncle, but, alas, he was only two months in London before he was returned to his mother and Pomony. Uncle was an engine-driver who disclosed to his astounded nephew a passion for gardening. This was incomprehensible to Johnny Flynn. A great roaring boiling locomotive was the grandest thing in the world. Johnny had rides on it, so he knew. And it was easy for him to imagine that every gardener cherished in the darkness of his disappointed soul an unavailing passion for a steam engine, but how an engine-driver could immerse himself in the mushiness of gardening was a baffling problem. However, before he returned home he discovered one important thing from his uncle's hobby, and he sent the information to his sister:

Dear Pomona,

Uncle Harry has got a alotment and grow veggutables. He says what makes the mold is worms. You know we puled all the worms out off our garden and chukked them over Miss Natchbols wall. Well you better get some more quick a lot ask George to help you and I bring som seeds home when I comes next week by the xcursion on Moms birthday

Your sincerely brother

John Flynn

On mother's birthday Pomona met him at the station. She kissed him shyly and explained that mother was going to have a half holiday to celebrate the double occasion and would be home with them at dinner time.

51

'Pomona, did you get them worms?'

Pomona was inclined to evade the topic of worms for the garden, but fortunately her brother's enthusiasm for another gardening project tempered the wind of his indignation. When they reached home he unwrapped two parcels he had brought with him; he explained his scheme to his sister; he led her into the garden. The Flynns' backyard, mostly paved with bricks, was small, and so the enclosing walls, truculently capped by chips of glass, although too low for privacy were yet too high for the growth of any cherishable plant. Johnny had certainly once reared a magnificent exhibit of two cowslips, but these had been mysteriously destroyed by the Knatchbole cat. The dank little enclosure was charged with sterility; nothing flourished there except a lot of beetles and a dauntless evergreen bush, as tall as Johnny, displaying a profusion of thick shiny leaves that you could split on your tongue and make squeakers with. Pomona showed him how to do this and they then busied themselves in the garden until the dinner siren warned them that mother would be coming home. They hurried into the kitchen and Pomona quickly spread the cloth and the plates of food upon the table, while Johnny placed conspicuously in the centre, after laboriously extracting the stopper with a fork and a hair-pin, a bottle of stout brought from London. He had been much impressed by numberless advertisements upon the hoardings respecting this attractive beverage. The children then ran off to meet their mother and they all came home together with great hilarity. Mrs. Flynn's attention having been immediately drawn to the sinister decoration of her dining table, Pomona was requested to pour out a glass of the nectar. Johnny handed this gravely to his parent, saying:

'Many happy returns of the day, Mrs. Flynn!'

'O dear, dear!' gasped his mother merrily, 'you drink first!'

'Excuse me, no, Mrs. Flynn,' rejoined her son, 'many happy returns of the day!'

When the toast had been honoured Pomona and Johnny looked tremendously at each other. 'Shall we?' exclaimed Pomona. 'Oh, yes,' decided Johnny; 'come on mum, in the garden, something marvellous!'

53

She followed her children into that dull little den, and by happy chance the sun shone grandly for the occasion. Behold, the dauntless evergreen bush had been stripped of its leaves and upon its blossomless twigs the children had hung numerous couples of ripe cherries, white and red and black.

'What do you think of it, mum?' they cried, snatching some of the fruit and pressing it into her hands, 'what do you think of it?'

'Beautiful!' replied Mrs. Flynn in a tremulous voice. The children stared silently at their mother until she could bear it no longer. She turned and went sobbing into the kitchen.

THE ELIXIR OF YOUTH

CHAPTER FOUR

The Elixir of Youth

*

Since the earth began its twisting, or since very soon after it began, there have been persons on it who perceived more or less early in life that it was seldom possible to get something in return for quite nothing, and that even if you did the delicate situation then arising was attended often with at least as much personal danger as delight, and generally with much more. Tom Toole knew all about it, so he was not going to sell his own little white soul to the devil, though he was sixty years of age and his soul, he expected, was shrivelled a bit now, like a dried fig. He had no faith in Wishing Hats, or Magic Carpets, or Herbs of Longevity, and he had not heard of the Philosopher's Stone, but he had a belief in an Elixir, somewhere in the world, that would make you young again. He had heard, too, of the Transmutation of Metals; indeed, he had associated himself a great many years ago with a Belfast brass-founder in the production of certain sovereigns. The brassfounder perished under the rigours of his subsequent incarceration in gaol, but Tom Toole had been not at all uncomfortable in the lunatic asylum to which a compassionate retribution had assigned him. It was in the asylum that he met the man from Kilsheelan who, if you could believe him, really had got a 'touch' from the fairies and could turn things he had no wish for into the things he would be wanting. The man from Kilsheelan first discovered his gift, so he told Tom Toole, when he caught a turtle-dove one day and changed it into a sheep. Then he turned the sheep into a lather-pot just to make sure and it *was* sure. So he thought he would like to go to the land of the Ever Young which is in the western country, but he did not know how he could get there unless he went in a balloon. Sure, he sat down in his cabin and turned the shaving-pot into a fine balloon, but the balloon was so large it burst down his house and he was brought to the asylum. Well that was clear enough to Tom Toole, and after he had got good advice from the man from Kilsheelan it came into his mind one day to slip out of the big gates of the asylum, and, believe me, since then he had walked the roads of Munster singing his ballads, and searching for something which was difficult to find, and that was his youth. For Tom Toole was growing old, a little old creature he was growing, gay enough and a bit of a philanderer still, but age is certain and puts the black teeth in your mouth and the whiteness of water on your hair.

One time he met a strange little old quick-talking man who came to him; he seemed just to bob up in front of him from the road itself.

'Ah, good day t'ye, and phwat part are ye from?'

'I'm from beyant,' said Tom Toole, nodding back to the Knockmealdown Mountains where the good monks had lodged him for a night.

'Ah, God deliver ye, and indeed I don't want to know your business at all but — but — where are ye going?'

Between his words he kept spitting, in six or seven little words there would be at least one spit. There was yellow dust in the flaps of his ears and neat bushes of hair in the holes. Cranks and wrinkles covered his nose, and the skull of him was bare, but there was a good tuft on his

59

chin. Tom Toole looked at him straight and queer for he did not admire the fierce expression of him, and there were smells of brimstone on him like a farmer who had been dipping his ewes, and he almost expected to see a couple of horns growing out of his brow.

'It's not meself does be knowing at all, good little man,' said Tom Toole to him, 'and I might go to the fair of Cappoquin, or I might walk on to Dungarvan, in the harbour now, to see will I buy a couple of lobsters for me nice supper.'

And he turned away to go off upon his road, but the little old man followed and kept by his side, telling him of a misfortune he had endured; a chaise of his, a little pony chaise, had been almost destroyed, but the ruin was not so great, for a kind lady of his acquaintance, a lady of his own denomination, had given him four pounds one shilling and ninepence. ' "Ah, not that I'm needing your money, ma'am," says I, "but damage is damage," I says, "and it's not right," I says, "that I should be at the harm of your coachman" '; and there he was spitting and going on like a clock spilling over its machinery when he unexpectedly grasped Tom Toole by the hand,

60

wished him Good day, and Good luck, and that he might meet him again —

Tom Toole walked on for an hour and came to a cross roads, and there was the same old man sitting in a neat little pony chaise smoking his pipe.

'Where are ye going?' says he.

'Dungarvan,' said Tom Toole.

'Jump in then,' said the little old man, and they jogged along the road conversing together; he was as sharp as an old goat.

'What is your aspiration?' he said, and Tom Toole told him.

'That's a good aspiration, indeed. I know what you're seeking Tom Toole; let's get on now and there'll be tidings in it.'

When Tom Toole and the little old man entered the public at Dungarvan they met a gang of strong young fellows, mechanics and people to drive the traction engines, for there was a circus in the town. Getting their fill of porter, they were, and nice little white loaves; very decent boys, but one of them a Scotchman with a large unrejoicing face, and he had a hooky nose with tussocks of hair in the nostrils and the two tails of hair to his moustache like an old Chinese man. Peter Mullane was telling a tale, and there was a sad bit of a man from Bristol with a sickness in his breast and a cough that would heave out the side of a mountain. Peter Mullane waited while Tom Toole and his friend sat down and then he proceeded with his tale.

'"Away with ye!" said the devil to Neal Carlin, and away he went to the four corners of the world. And when he came to the first corner he saw a place where the rivers do be rushing –'

'– the only damn thing that does rush then in this country,' interrupted the Scotchman with a sneer.

'Shut your –' began the man from Bristol, but he was taken with the cough, until his cheeks were scarlet and his eyes, fixed angrily upon the Highland man, were strained to tear-drops. 'Shut your –' he began it again, but he was rent by a large and vexing spasm that rocked him, while his friends looked at him and wondered would he be long for this world. He recovered quite suddenly and exclaimed, '– damn face' to that Highland man. And then Peter Mullane went on:

'I am not given to thinking,' said he, 'that the Lord would put a country the like of Ireland in a wee corner of the world, and he wanting the nook of it for thistles and the poor savages that devour them. Well, Neal Carlin came to a place where the rivers do be rushing –' he paused invitingly, 'and he saw a little fairy creature with fine tresses of hair sitting under a rowan tree.'

'A rowan?' exclaimed the Highland man.

Peter nodded.

'A Scottish tree!' declared the other.

'O shut your –' began the little coughing man, but again his conversation was broken, and by the time he had recovered from his spasms the company was mute.

'If,' said Peter Mullane, 'you'd wish to observe the rowan in its pride and beauty just clap your eye upon it in the Galtee Mountains. How would it thrive, I ask you, in a place which was stiff with granite and sloppy with haggis? And what would ye do, my clever man, what would ye do, if ye met a sweet fairy woman –?'

'I'd kiss the Judy,' said the Highland man, spitting a great splash.

63

Peter Mullane gazed at him for a minute or two as if he did not love him much.

'Neal Carlin was attracted by her, she was a sweet creature. "Warm!" says she to him with a friendly tone. "Begod, ma'am, it is a hot day," he said, and thinks he, she is a likely person to give me my aspiration. And sure enough when he sat down beside her she asked him, "What is your aspiration, Neal Carlin?" and he said, "Saving your grace, ma'am, it is but to enjoy the world and to be easy in it." "That is a good aspiration," she said, and she gave him some secret advice. He went home to his farm, Neal Carlin did, and he followed the advice, and in a month or two he had grown very wealthy, and things were easy with him. But still he was not satisfied, he had a greedy mind, and his farm looked a drifty little place that was holding him down from big things. So he was not satisfied though things were easy with him, and one night before he went sleeping he made up his mind. "It's too small it is. I'll go away from it now and a farm twice as big I will have, three times as big, yes, I will have it ten times as big." He went sleeping on the wilderness of his avarice, and when he rolled off the settle in the morning and stood up to stretch his limbs he hit his head a wallop against the rafter. He cursed it and had a kind of thought that the place had got smaller. As he went from the door he struck his brow against the lintel hard enough to beat down the house. What is come to me, he roared in his pains; and looking into his field there were his five cows and his bullock no bigger than sheep – will ye believe that, then – and his score of ewes no bigger than rabbits, mind it now, and it was not all, for the very jackdaws were no bigger than chafers and the neat little wood was no more account than a grove of raspberry bushes. Away he goes to the surgeon's to have drops put in his eyes for he feared the blindness was coming on him, but on his return there was his bullock no bigger than an old boot, and his cabin had wasted to the size of a bird-cage.'

Peter leaned forward, for the boys were quiet, and consumed a deal of porter. And the Highland man asked him, 'Well, what happened?'

'Oh, he just went up to his cabin and kicked it over the hedge as you might an old can, and then he strolled off to another corner of the world, Neal Carlin did, whistling "The Lanty Girl." '

Tom Toole's friend spoke to Peter Mullane. 'Did ye say it was in the Galtee Mountains that the young fellow met the lady?'

'In the Galtee Mountains,' said Peter.

'To the Galtee Mountains let us be going, Tom Toole,' cried the little old man, 'Come on now, there'll be tidings in it!'

So off they drove, and when they had driven a day and slept a couple of nights they were there, and they came to a place where the rivers do be rushing, and there was a rowan tree, but no lady on it.

'What will we do now, Tom Toole?' says the old man.

'We'll not stint it,' says he, and they searched by night and by day looking for a person who would give them their youth again. They sold the chaise for some guineas and the pony for a few more, and they were walking among the hills for a thousand days, but never a dust of fortune did they discover. Whenever they asked a person to guide them they would be swearing at them or they would jeer.

66

'Well, may a good saint stretch your silly old skins for ye!' said one.

'Thinking of your graves and travelling to the priest ye should be!' said one.

'The nails of your boots will be rusty and rotten searching for the like of that,' said one.

'It's two quarts of black milk from a Kerry cow ye want,' said one; 'take a sup of that and you'll be young again!'

'Of black milk,' said Tom Toole's friend, 'where would you get that?'

The person said he would get a pull of it in the Comeragh Mountains, fifty miles away.

'Tom Toole,' said the little old man, 'it's what I'll do. I'll walk on to the Comeragh Mountains to see what I will see, and do you go on searching here, for to find that young girl would be better than forty guineas' worth of blather. And when I find the cow I'll take my fill of a cup and bring you to it.'

So they agreed upon it and the old man went away saying, 'I'll be a score of days no more. Good day, Tom Toole, good day!' much as an old crow might shout it to a sweep.

When he was gone Tom Toole journeyed

about the world, and the day after he went walking to a fair. Along the road the little ass carts were dribbling into town from Fews and Carrigleena, when he saw a young girl in a field trying to secure an ass.

'Oi –, Oi –!' the girl was calling out to him, and he went in the field and helped her with the ass, which was a devil to capture, and it not wanting. She thanked him; she was a sweet slip of a colleen with a long fall of hair that the wind was easy with.

''Tis warm!' she said to Tom Toole. 'Begod, ma'am,' says he to her quickly, taking his cue, 'it is a hot day.'

'Where are ye going, Tom Toole,' she asked him, and he said:

'I am seeking a little contrivance, ma'am, that will let me enjoy the world and live easy in it. That is my aspiration.'

'I'll give you what you are seeking,' and she gave him a wee bottle with red juices in it.

'Indeed, ma'am, I'm obliged to ye,' and he took her by the hand and wished her Good day and Good luck, and that he might meet her again.

68

When he got the elixir of youth he gave over his searching. He hid the bottle in his breast and went up into the mountains as high as he could go to bide the coming of the little old man. It is a queer thing but Tom Toole had never heard the name of him — it would be some place in the foreign corners of the world, like Portugal, that he had come from no doubt. Up he went; first there was rough pasture for bullocks, then fern and burnt furze, and then little but heather, and great rocks strewn about like shells, and sour brown streams coming from the bog. He wandered about for twenty days and the old man did not return, and for forty days he was still alone. 'The divil receive him, but I'll die against his return!' And Tom Toole pulled the wee bottle from his breast. He was often minded to lift the cork and take a sup of the elixir of youth. 'But,' says he, 'it would be an unfriendly deed. Sure if I got me youth sudden I'd be off to the wonders of the land and leave that old fool roaming till the Day of Judgment,' and he would put the bottle away and wait for scores of days until he was sick and sorry with grieving. A thousand days he was on his lonely wanderings, soft days as mellow as cream, and hard days when it is ribs of iron itself you would want to stiffen you against the crack of the blast. His skimpy hair grew down to the lappet of his coat, very ugly he was, but the little stranger sheep of the mountain were not daunted when he moved by, and even the flibeens had the soft call for him. A thousand days was in it, and then he said:

'Good evening to my good luck. I've had my enough of this. Sure I'll despise myself for evermore if I wait the tide of another drifting day. It's to-night I'll sleep in a neat bed with a quilt of down over me heart, for I'm going to be young again.'

He crept down the mountain to a neat little town and went in a room in the public to have a cup of porter. A little forlorn old man also came in from the road and sat down beside, and when they looked at each other they each let out a groan. 'Glory be!' says he. 'Glory be,' cried Tom Toole, 'it's the good little man in the heel of it. Where are ye from?'

'From the mountains.'

'And what fortune is in it? Did ye find the farm?'

'Divil a clod.'

'Nor the Kerry cow?'

'Divil a horn.'

'Nor the good milk?'

'Divil a quart, and I that dry I could be drunk with the smell of it. Tom Toole, I have traipsed the high and the deep of this realm and believe you me it is not in it; the long and the wide of this realm – not in it.' He kept muttering sadly, 'Not in it.'

'Me good little man,' cried Tom Toole, 'don't be havering like an old goat. Here it is! the fortune of the world!'

He took the wee bottle from his breast and shook it before his eyes. 'The drops that 'ull give ye your youth as easy as shifting a shirt. Come, now, I've waited the long days to share wid ye, for I couldn't bring myself to desart a comrade who was ranging the wild regions for the likes of me. Many's the time I've lifted the cork, and thinks I: he's gone and soon I'll be going, so here goes. Divil a go was it. I could not do it, not for silver and not for gold, and not for all the mad raging mackerel that sleep in the sea.'

71

The little old stranger took the wee bottle in his two hands. He was but a quavering stick of a man now; half dead he was, and his name it is Martin O'Moore.

'Is it the rale stuff, Tom Toole?'

'From herself I got it,' he said, and he let on to him about that sweet spoken girl.

'Did she give you the directions on the head of it?'

'What directions is it?'

'The many drops is a man to drink!'

'No, but a good sup of it will do the little job.'

'A good sup of it Tom Toole, a good sup of it, ay?' says he, unsqueezing the cork. 'The elixir of youth, a good sup of it, says you, a good sup of it, a great good good sup of it!'

And sticking it into his mouth he drained the wee bottle of its every red drop. He stood there looking like a man in a fit, holding the empty bottle in his hand until Tom Toole took it from him with reproaches in his poor old eyes. But in a moment it was his very eyes he thought were deceiving him; not an inch of his skin but had the dew of fear on it, for the little old man began to change his appearance quick like the sand running through a glass or as fast as the country changes down under a flying swan.

'Mother o' God!' screamed Martin O'Moore, 'it's too fast backward I'm growing; dizzy, dizzy I am.'

And indeed his bald head suddenly got the fine black hair grown upon it, the whiskers flew away from him and his face was young. He began to wear a strange old suit, that suddenly got new, and he had grown down through a handsome pair of trousers and into the little knickerbockers of a boy before you could count a score. And he had a bit of a cold just then, though he was out of it in a twink, and he let a sneeze that burst a button off his breeches, a little tin button, which was all that ever was found of him. Smaller and smaller he fell away, like the dust in an hour glass, till he was no bigger than an acorn, and then devil a bit of him was left there at all.

Tom Toole was frightened at the quiet and the emptiness and he made to go away, but he turned in the doorway and stretching out his arms to the empty room he whispered, 'The greed, the avarice, may hell pour all its buckets on your bad little heart! May –' But just then he caught sight of the cup of porter that Martin O'Moore had forgotten to drink, so he went back to drink his enough and then went out into the great roaring world where he walked from here to there until one day he came right back to his old asylum. He had been away for twenty years, he was an old man, very old indeed. And there was the man from Kilsheelan digging potatoes just inside the gates of the sunny garden.

'Tis warm!' said the traveller staring at him through the railings, but the man from Kilsheelan only said, "Come in, Tom Toole, is it staying or going ye are?'

FELIX TINCLER

CHAPTER FIVE

Felix Tincler

*

THE child was to have a birthday to-morrow and was therefore not uneasy about being late home from school this afternoon. He had lost his pencil case, a hollow long round thing it was, like a rolling-pin, only it had green and yellow rings painted upon it. He kept his marbles in it and so he was often in a trouble about his pencils. He had not tried very much to find the pencil case because the boys 'deludered' him — that's what his father always said. He had asked Heber Gleed if he had seen it — he had strange suspicions of that boy — but Heber Gleed had sworn so earnestly that the greengrocer opposite the school had picked it up, he had even 'saw him do it,' that Felix Tincler went into Mr. Gobbit's shop, and when the greengrocer lady appeared in answer to the ring of the door bell he enquired politely for his pencil case. She was tall and terrible with a squint and, what was worse, a large velvety mole with hairs sprouting from it. She immediately and with inexplicable

fury desired him to flee from her greengrocer
shop, with a threat of alternative castigation in
which a flat iron and a red-hot pick-axe were to
figure with unusual and unpleasant prominence.
Well, he had run out of Mr. Gobbit's shop and
there was Heber Gleed standing in the road
giggling derisively at him. Felix walked on
alone looking in the gutters and areas for his
pencil case until he encountered another friendly
boy who took him to dig in a garden where they
grew castor-oil plants. When he went home it
was late; as he ran along under the high wall
of the orphanage that occupied one end of his
street its harsh peevish bell clanged out six notes.
He scampered past the great gateway under the
dismal arch that always filled him with uneasiness, he never passed it without feeling the sad
trouble that a prison might give. He stepped
into his own pleasant home, a little mute, and
a little dirty in appearance; but at six years of
age in a home so comfortable and kind the eve
of the day that is to turn you into seven is an
occasion great enough to yield an amnesty for
peccadilloes. His father was already in from
work, he could hear him singing. He gave his

mother the sprigs he had picked from the castor-oil plant and told her about the pencil case. The meal was laid upon the table, and while mother was gone into the kitchen to boil the water for tea he sat down and tried to smooth out the stiff creases in the white table cloth. His father was singing gaily in the scullery as he washed and shaved:

High cockalorum,
Charlie ate the spinach . . .

He ceased for a moment to give the razor a vigorous stropping and then continued:

High cockalorum,
High cockalee . . .

Felix knew that was not the conclusion of the song. He listened, but for some moments all that followed was the loud crepitation of a razor searching a stubborn beard and the sigh of the kettle. Then a new vigour seized the singer:

But mother brought the pandy down
And bate the gree . . .

Again that rasping of chin briefly intervened,

but the conclusion of the cropping was soon denoted by the strong rallentando of the singer:

> *. . . dy image,*
> *High cock – alorum,*
> *High cock – a – lee.*

Mrs. Tincler brought in the teapot and her husband followed her with his chin tightly shaven but blue, crying with mock horror:

'Faylix, my son! that is seven years old to-morrow! look at him, Mary, the face of him and the hands of him! I didn't know there was a bog in this parish; is it creeping in a bog you have been?'

The boy did not blench at his father's spurious austerity, he knew he was the soul of kindness and fun.

'Go wash yourself at the sink,' interposed his mother. Kevin Tincler, taking his son by the hand, continued with mocking admonishment: 'All the fine copybooks of the world that you've filled up with that blather about cleanliness and holiness, the up strokes very thin and the down strokes very thick! What was it, Mary, he has let it all out of his mind?'

'Go and wash, Felix, and come quickly and have your tea,' laughed Mary Tincler.

'Ah, but what was it – in that grand book of yours?'

The boy stood, in his short buff tunic, regarding his father with shy amusement. The small round clear-skinned face was lovely with its blushes of faint rose; his eyes were big and blue, and his head was covered with thick curling locks of rich brown hair.

'Cleanliness comes next to godliness,' he replied.

'Does it so, indeed?' exclaimed his father. 'Then you're putting your godliness in a pretty low category!'

'What a nonsense,' said Mary Tincler as the boy left them.

The Irishman and his dark-eyed Saxon wife sat down at the table waiting for their son.

'There's a bit of a randy in the Town Gardens to-night, Mary, dancing on the green, fireworks! When the boy is put to bed we'll walk that way.'

Mary expressed her pleasure, but then declared she could not leave the boy alone in his bed.

'He'll not hurt, Mary, he has no fear in him.
Give him the birthday gift before we go. Whisht,
he's coming!'

The child, now clean and handsome, came to
his chair and looked up at his father sitting
opposite to him.

'Holy Mother!' exclaimed the admiring
parent, 'it's the neck of a swan he has. Faylix
Tincler, may you live to be the father of a
bishop!'

After tea his father took him upon the downs
for an hour. As they left their doorway a group
of the tidy but wretched orphans was marching
back into their seminary, little girls moving in
double columns behind a stiff-faced woman.
They were all dressed alike in garments of
charity, exact as pilchards. Grey capes, worsted
stockings, straw hats with blue bands round
them, and hard boots. The boys were coming in
from a different direction, but all of them, even
the minutest, were clad in corduroy trousers and
short jackets high throated like a gaoler's. This
identity of garment was contrary to the will of
God, for he had certainly made their pinched
bodies diverse enough. Some were short, some

tall, dark, fair, some ugly, others handsome. The sight of them made Felix unhappy, he shrank into himself, until he and his father had slipped through a gap in a hedge and were going up the hill that stretched smoothly and easily almost from their very door. The top of the down hereabouts was quiet and lovely, but a great flank of it two miles away was scattered over with tiny white figures playing very deliberately at cricket. Pleasant it was up there in the calm evening, and still bright, but the intervening valley was full of grey ungracious houses, allotments, railway arches, churches, graveyards, and schools. Worst of all was the dull forbidding aspect of the Orphanage down beyond the roof of their own house.

They played with a ball and had some wrestling matches until the declining day began to grow dim even on the hill and the fat jumbo clouds over the town were turning pink. If those elephants fell on him – what would they do? Why they'd mix him up like ice-cream! So said his father.

'Do things ever fall out of the sky?'

'Rain,' said Mr. Tincler.

'Yes, I know.'

' Stars – maybe.'

'Where do they go?'

'Oh, they drop on the hills but ye can never find 'em.'

'Don't Heaven ever?'

'What, drop down! No,' said Mr. Tincler, 'it don't. I have not heard of it doing that, but maybe it all just stoops down sometimes, Faylix, until it's no higher than the crown of your hat. Let us be going home now and ye'll see something this night.'

'What is it?'

'Wait, Faylix, wait!'

As they crossed from the hill Mary, drawing down the blinds, signalled to them from the window.

'Come along, Felix,' she cried, and the child ran into the darkened room. Upon the table was set a little church of purest whiteness. Kevin had bought it from an Italian hawker. It had a wonderful tall steeple and a cord that came through a hole and pulled a bell inside. And that was not all; the church was filled with light that was shining through a number of tiny arched windows, blue, purple, green, violet, the wonderful windows were everywhere. Felix was silent with wonder; how could you get a light in a church that hadn't a door! Then Mary lifted the hollow building from the table; it had no floor, and there was a nightlight glowing in one of her patty-pans filled with water. The church was taken up to bed with him in the small chamber next his parents' room and set upon a bureau. Kevin and Mary then went off to the 'bit of devilment' in the town gardens.

Felix kept skipping from his bed, first to gaze at the church, and then to lean out of the window in his night-shift, looking for the lamplighter who would come to the street lamp outside. The house was the very last and the lamp was the very last one on the roads that led from the town and went poking out into the steady furze-covered downs. And as the lamp was the very last to be lit darkness was always half-fallen by the time the old man arrived at his journey's end. He carried a pole with a brass tube on its top. There were holes in the brass tube show-ing gleams of light. The pole rested upon his shoulders as he trudged along, humming huskily.

'Here he is,' cried Felix, leaning from the window and waving a white arm. The dull road, empty of traffic, dim as his mother's pantry by day, curved slightly, and away at the other end of the curve a jet of light had sprung into the gloom like a bright flower bursting its sheath; a black figure moved along towards him under the Orphanage wall. Other lamps blossomed with light and the lamplighter, approaching the Tinclers' lamp, thrust the end of his pole into the lantern, his head meanwhile craning back like the head of a horse that has been pulled violently backwards. He deftly turned the tap; with a tiny dull explosion that sounded like a doormat being beaten against the wall in the next street the lamp was lit and the face of the old man sprang into vague brilliance, for it was not yet utterly dark. Vague as the light was, the neighbouring hills at once faded out of recognition and became black bulks of oblivion.

'Oi . . . Oi . . .' cried the child, clapping his hands. The old man's features relaxed, he grunted in relief, the pole slid down in his palm. As the end of it struck the pavement a sharp knock he drew an old pipe from his pocket and lit it quite easily, although one of his hands was deficient of a thumb and some fingers. He was about to travel back into the sparkling town when Felix called to him:

'Soloman! Soloman!'

'Goo an to yer bed, my little billycock, or you'll ketch a fever.'

'No, but what's this?' Felix was pointing to the ground below him. The old man peered over the iron railings into the front garden that had just sufficient earth to cherish four deciduous bushes, two plants of marigold, and some indeterminate herbs. In the dimness of their shadows a glowworm beamed clearly.

'That?' exclaimed he; 'Oh, s'dripped off the moon, yas, right off, moon's wasting away, you'll see later on if you'm watch out for it, s'dripped off the moon, right off.' Chuckling, he blew out the light at the end of his pole, and went away, but turned at intervals to wave his hand towards the sky, crying 'Later on, right off!' and cackling genially until he came to a tavern.

The child stared at the glowworm and then surveyed the sky, but the tardy moon was deep behind the hills. He left the open window and climbed into bed again. The house was empty, but he did not mind, father and mother had gone to buy him another birthday gift. He did not mind, the church glowed in its corner on the bureau, the street lamp shined all over the ceiling and a little bit upon the wall where the splendid picture of Wexford Harbour was hanging. It was not gloomy at all, although the Orphanage bell once sounded very piercingly. Sometimes people would stroll by, but not often, and he would hear them mumbling to each other. He would rather have a Chinese lantern first, and next to that a little bagpipe, and next to that a cockatoo with a yellow head, and then a Chinese lantern, and then. . . . He awoke; he thought he heard a heavy bang on the door as if somebody had thrown a big stone. But when he looked out of the window there was nobody to be seen. The little moon-drip was still lying in the dirt, the sky was softly black, the stars were vivid, only the lamp dazzled his eyes and he could not see any moon. But as he yawned he saw just over the downs a rich globe of light moving very gradually towards him, swaying and falling, falling in the still air. To the child's dazzled eyes the great globe, dropping towards him as if it would crush the house, was shaped like an elephant, a fat squat jumbo with a green trunk. Then to his relief it fell suddenly from the sky right on to the down where he and father had played. The light was extinguished and black night hid the fire-balloon.

He scrambled back into bed again, but how he wished it was morning so that he could go out and capture the old elephant – he knew he would find it! When at last he slept he sank into a world of white churches that waved their steeples like vast trunks, and danced with elephants that had bellies full of fire and hidden bells that clanged impetuously to a courageous pull of each tail. He did not wake again until morning was bright and birds were singing. It was early, but it was his birthday. There were no noises in the street yet, and he could not hear his father or mother moving about. He crawled silently from his bed and dressed himself. The coloured windows in the little white fane gleamed still but it looked a little dull now. He took the cake that mother always left at his bedside and crept down the stairs. There he put on his shoes and, munch-

ing the cake, tiptoed to the front door. It was
not bolted, but it was difficult for him to slip
back the latch quietly, and when at last it was
done and he stood upon the step he was doubly
startled to hear a loud rapping on the knocker
of a house a few doors away. He sidled quickly
but warily to the corner of the street, crushing
the cake into his pocket, and then peeped back.
It was more terrible than he had anticipated! A
tall policeman stood outside that house, bawling
to a woman with her hair in curl papers who was
lifting the sash of an upper window. Felix
turned and ran through the gap in the hedge and
onwards up the hill. He did not wait; he thought
he heard the policeman calling out 'Tincler!'
and he ran faster and faster, then slower and
more slow as the down steepened, until he was
able to sink down breathless behind a clump of
the furze, out of sight and out of hearing. The
policeman did not appear to be following him;
he moved on up the hill and through the soft
smooth alleys of the furze until he reached the
top of the down, searching always for the white
elephant which he knew must be hidden close
there and nowhere else, although he had no clear

idea in his mind of the appearance of his mysterious quarry. Vain search, the elephant was shy
or cunning and eluded him. Hungry at last and
tired he sat down and leaned against a large ant
hill close beside the thick and perfumed furze.
Here he ate his cake and then lolled, a little
drowsy, looking at the few clouds in the sky and
listening to birds. A flock of rooks was moving
in straggling flight towards him, a wide flat
changing skein, like a curtain of crape that was
being pulled and stretched delicately by invisible
fingers. One of the rooks flapped just over him;
it had a small round hole right through the
feathers of one wing – what was that for? Felix
was just falling to sleep, it was so soft and comfortable there, when a tiny noise, very tiny but
sharp and mysterious, went 'Ping!' just by his
ear, and something stung him lightly in the
neck. He knelt up, a little startled, but he peered
steadily under the furze. 'Ping!' went something
again and stung him in the ball of the eye. It
made him blink. He drew back; after staring
silently at the furze he said very softly, 'Come
out!' Nothing came; he beckoned with his fore-
finger and called aloud with friendliness, 'come

on, come out!' At that moment his nose was
almost touching a brown dry sheath of the furze
bloom, and right before his eyes the dried flower
burst with the faint noise of 'Ping!' and he felt
the shower of tiny black seeds shooting against
his cheek. At once he comprehended the charming mystery of the furze's dispersal of its seeds,
and he submitted himself to the fairylike
bombardment with great glee, forgetting even
the elephant until in one of the furze alleys he
came in sight of a heap of paper that fluttered
a little heavily. He went towards it; it was so
large that he could not make out its shape or
meaning. It was a great white bag made of
paper, all crumpled and damp, with an arrangement of wire where the hole was, and some
burned tow fixed in it. But at last he was able to
perceive the green trunk, and it also had pink
eyes! He had found it and he was triumphant!
There were words in large black letters painted
upon it which he could not read, except one word
which was CURE. It was an advertisement fire-
balloon relating to a specific for catarrh. He
rolled the elephant together carefully, and carrying the mass of it clasped in his two arms he ran

back along the hill chuckling to himself, 'I'm carrying the ole elephant.' Advancing down the hill to his home he was precariously swathed in a drapery of balloon paper. The door stood open; he walked into the kitchen. No one was in the kitchen, but there were sharp straight voices speaking in the room above. He thought he must have come into the wrong house, but the strange noises frightened him into silence; he stood quite still listening to them. He had dropped the balloon and it unfolded upon the floor, partly revealing the astounding advertisement of

PEASEGOOD'S PODOPHYLLIN

The voices above were unravelling horror upon horror. He knew by some divining instinct that tragedy was happening to him, had indeed already enveloped and crushed him. A mortar had exploded at the fireworks display, killing and wounding people that he knew.

'She had a great hole of a wound in the soft part of her thigh as you could put a cokernut in . . .'

'God a'mighty . . .'

'Died in five minutes, poor thing.'

93

'And the husband . . . they couldn't . . .?'

'No, couldn't identify . . . they could not identify him . . . only by some papers in his pocket.'

'And he'd got a little bagpipe done up in a package . . . for their little boy . . .'

'Never spoke a word. . . .'

'Never a word, poor creature.'

'May Christ be good to 'em.'

'Yes, yes,' they all said softly.

The child walked quietly up the stairs to his mother's bedroom. Two policemen were there making notes in their pocket books, their helmets lying on the unused bed. There were also three or four friendly women neighbours. As he entered the room the gossip ceased abruptly. One of the women gasped 'O Jesus!' and they seemed to huddle together, eyeing him as if he had stricken them with terror. With his fingers still upon the handle of the door he looked up at the taller policeman and said:

'What's the matter?'

The policeman did not reply immediately; he folded up his notebook, but the woman who had gasped came to him with a yearning cry and wrapped him in her protesting arms with a thousand kisses.

'Ye poor lamb, ye poor little orphan, whatever 'ull become of ye!'

At that moment the bell of the Orphanage burst into a peal of harsh impetuous clangour and the policemen picked up their helmets from the bed.

CRAVEN ARMS

G

CHAPTER SIX

Craven Arms

*

ALL schools since the beginning of time have been modern at some period of their existence, but this one was modern, so the vicar declared, because it was so blessedly hygienic; the townspeople were perhaps proudest of its evening classes, very advanced they were – languages, sciences, arts – and very popular. The school was built upon a high tree-arboured slope overlooking the snug small town and on its western side stared ambiguously at a free upland country that was neither small nor snug. The seventeen young women and the nine young men who comprised the evening sketching class were definitely, indeed articulately, inartistic; they were as unæsthetic as pork pies, all except Julia Tern, a golden-haired pure-complexioned fawn of a girl whose talent was already beyond the reach of any instruction the teacher could give. He could not understand why she continued to attend his classes.

One evening she brought for his criticism a portrait sketch of himself.

'This is extraordinarily beautiful,' he murmured.

'Yes,' said Julia.

'I mean the execution, the presentation and so on.'

Julia did not reply. He stared at her picture of him, a delicately modelled face with a suggestion of nobility, an air that was kind as it was grave. The gravity and nobility which so pleased him were perhaps the effect of a high brow from which the long brown hair flowed thinly back to curve in a tidy cluster at his neck. Kindness beamed in the eyes and played around the thin mouth, sharp nose and positive chin. What could have inspired her to make this idealisation of himself, for it was idealisation in spite of its fidelity and likeness? He knew he had little enough nobility of character – too little to show so finely – and as for that calm gravity of aspect, why gravity simply was not in him. But there it was on paper, deliberate and authentic, inscribed with his name – *David Masterman* 1912.

'When, how, did you come to do it?'

'I just wanted it, you were a nice piece, I watched you a good deal, and there you are!' She said it jauntily, but there was a pink flush on her cheeks.

'It's delicious,' he mused, 'I envy you. I can't touch a decent head – not even yours. But why have you idealised me so?' He twitted her lightly about the gravity and nobility.

'But you are like that, you are. That's how I see you at this moment.'

She did not give him the drawing as he hoped she would. He did not care to ask her for it – there was delicious flattery in the thought that she treasured it so much.

Masterman was a rather solitary man of about thirty. He lived alone in a bungalow away out of the town, and painted numbers of landscapes, rather lifeless imitations, as he knew, of other men's masterpieces. They were frequently sold.

Sometimes on summer afternoons he would go into woods or fields with a few of his pupils to sketch or paint farmhouses, trees, clouds, stacks, and other rural furniture. He was always hoping to sit alone with Julia Tern; but there were other loyal pupils who never missed these occasions, among them the two Forrest girls, Ianthe, the younger, and Katherine, daughters of a thriving contractor. Julia remained inscrutable, she gave him no opportunities at all: he could never divine her feelings or gather any response to his own, but there could be no doubt of the feelings of the Forrest girls – they quite certainly liked him, liked him enormously, and indeed could have had no other reason for continuing in his classes, both being as devoid of artistic grace as an inkstand. They brought fruit or chocolate to the classes and shared them with him. Their attentions, their mutual attentions, were manifested in many ways, small but signific-ant and kind. On such occasions Julia's eyes seemed to rest upon him with an ironical gaze. It was absurd. He liked them well enough and sometimes from his shy wooing of the adorable but enigmatic Julia he would turn for solace to Ianthe. Yet strangely enough it was Kate, the least alluring to him of the three girls, who took him to her melancholy heart.

Ianthe was a little bud of womanhood, dark-haired but light-headed, dressed in cream-coloured clothes. She was small and right and tight, without angularities or rhythms, just one dumpy solid roundness. But she had an extraordinary vulgarity of speech, if not of mind, that exacerbated him, and in the dim corridors of his imagination she did not linger; she scurried as it were into doorways or upon twisting staircases or stood briefly where a loop of light fell upon her hair, her dusky face, her creamy clothes and her delightful rotundities. She had eyes of indiscretion and a mind like a hive of bees, it had such a tiny opening and was so full of a cloying content.

One day he suddenly found himself alone with Ianthe in a glade of larch trees which they had all been sketching. They had loitered. He had been naming wild flowers which Ianthe had picked for the purpose and then thrown wantonly away. She spied a single plant of helleborine growing in the dimness under the closely planted saplings.

'Don't! Don't!' he cried. He kept her from plucking it and they knelt down together to admire the white virginal flower. His arm fell around Ianthe's waist in a light casual way. He scarcely realised its presumption. He had not intended to do it; as far as that went he did not particularly want to do it, but there his arm was. Ianthe took no notice of the embrace and he felt foolish, he could not retreat until they rose to walk on; then Ianthe pressed close to his side until his arm once more stole round her.

'Heavens above,' she said, 'you do get away with it quick!'

'Life's short, there's no time to lose, I do as I'd be done by.'

'And there are so many of us! But glory,' said the jolly girl, taking him to her bosom, 'in for a penny, in for a pound.'

She did not pick any more flowers, and soon they were out of the wood, decorously joining the others. He imagined that Julia's gaze was full of irony, the timid wonder in Kate's eyes moved him uncomfortably, there was something idiotic in the whole affair.

Until the end of the summer he met Ianthe often enough in the little town or in the city three miles further off. Her uncouthness still re-pelled him and sometimes he disliked her completely, but she was always happy to be with him, fond and gay with all the endearing alertness of a pert bird.

Her sister Kate was not just the mere female that Ianthe was; at once sterner and softer her passions were more strong but their defences stood solid as a rock. In spite of her reserve she was always on the brink of her emotions, and they, unhappily for her, were often not transient, but enduring. She was nearly thirty, still un-wed. Her dark beauty, for she, too, was fine, seemed to brood in melancholy over his attentions to the other two women. She was quiet, she had little to say, she seemed to stand and wait.

One autumn night after the pupils had gone home from school he walked into the dim lobby for his hat and coat. Kate Forrest was there. She stood with her back to him adjusting her hat. She did not say a word, nor did he address her. They were almost touching each other, there was a pleasant scent about her. In the class-room behind the caretaker was walking about the hollow sounding floor, humming loudly as he clapped down windows and mounted the six chairs to turn out the six gas lamps.

When the last light through the glazed door
was gone and the lobby was completely dark
Kate all at once turned to him, folded him in her
arms, and held him to her breast for one startling
moment, then let him go, murmuring 'Oh . . .
Oh.' It made him strangely happy. He pulled
her back in the gloom, whispering tender words.
They walked out of the hall into the dark road
and stopped to confront each other. The road
was empty and dark except for a line of gas
lamps that gleamed piercingly bright in the sharp
air and in the polished surface of the road that
led back from the hill down past her father's
villa. There were no lamps in the opposite direction and the road groped its way out into the
dark country where he lived, a mile beyond the
town. It was windy and some unseen trees
behind a wall near them swung and tossed with
many pleasant sounds.

'I will come a little way with you,' Kate said.
'Yes, come a little way,' he whispered, pressing her arm. 'I'll come back with you.'

She took his arm and they turned towards the
country. He could think of nothing to say, he
was utterly subdued by his surprise: Kate was

sad, even moody; but at last she said slowly: 'I am unlucky. I always fall in love with men who can't love me.'

'Oh, but I can and do, dear Kate,' he cried lightly, 'love me, Kate, go on loving me, I'm not, well, I'm not very wicked.'

'No, no, you do not.' She shook her head mournfully; after a few moments she added: 'It's Julia Tern.'

That astonished him too. How could she have known it! How could anyone have known – even Julia herself? It was queer that she did not refer to his friendship with Ianthe; he thought that was much more obvious than his love for Julia. In a mood that he only half understood he began to deny her reproachful charge. 'Why, you must think me very fickle indeed. I really love you, dear Kate, really you.'

His arm was around her neck, he smoothed her cheek fondly against his own. She returned his caresses, but he could glimpse the melancholy doubt in her averted eyes.

'We often talk of you, we often talk of you at night in bed, often.'

'What do you say about me – in bed? Who?'

107

'Ianthe and me. She likes you.'

'She likes me! What do you say about me – in bed?'

He hoped Ianthe had not been indiscreet, but Kate only said: 'She doesn't like you as I do – not like this.'

Soon they began to walk back towards the town. He smiled once when, as their footsteps clattered irregularly upon the hard clean road, she skipped to adjust the fall of her steps to his.

'Do not come any further,' she begged, as they neared the street lamps. 'It doesn't matter, not at all, what I've said to you. It will be all right. I shall see you again.'

Once more she put her arms around his neck, murmuring 'Good-night, good-night, good-night.'

He watched her go quietly away. When he turned homeward his mind was full of thoughts that were only dubiously pleasant. It was all right, surprisingly sweet, but it left him uneasy. He managed to light a cigarette, but the wind blew smoke into his eyes, tore the charred end into fiery rags, and tossed the sparkles across his

108

shoulder. If it had only been Julia Tern! – or even Ianthe! – he would have been wholly happy. Kate was good-looking, but these quietly passionate advances disturbed him. Why had he been so responsive to her? He excused himself, it was quite simple; you could not let a woman down, a loving woman like that, not at once, a man should be kind. But what did she mean when he spoke of always falling in love with men who did not like her?

He tossed the cigarette away and turned up the collar of his coat, for the faintest fall of warm rain blew against his face like a soft beautiful net. He thrust his hands into his pockets and walked sharply and forgettingly home.

2

Three miles away from the little town was the big city with tramways, electric light, factories, canals, and tens of thousands of people, and there a few nights later he met Ianthe. Walking around and away from the happy lighted streets they came out upon the bank of a canal where darkness and loneliness were intensified by the silent passage of black water whose current they could define but not see. As they stepped warily along the unguarded bank he embraced her. Even as he did so he cursed himself for a fool to be so fond of this wretched imp of a girl. In his heart he believed he disliked her, but he was not sure. She was childish, artful, luscious, stupid – this was no gesture for a man with any standards. Silently clutching each other they approached an iron bridge with lamps upon it and a lighted factory beyond it. The softly-moving water could now be seen; the lamps on the bridge let down thick rods of light into its quiet depths, and beyond the arch the windows of the factory, inverted in the stream, bloomed like baskets of fire with flaming fringes. A boy shuffled across the bridge whistling a tune; there was the distant rumble and trot of a cab. Then all sounds melted into quiet without one wave of air. Ianthe was replying to him:

'No, no, I like it, I like you.' She put her brow against his breast: 'I like you, I like you.'

His embracing hand could feel the emotion streaming within the girl.

'Do you like me better than her?'

'Than whom?' he asked.

Ianthe was coy. 'You know, you know.'

Masterman's feelings were a mixture of perturbation and delight, delight at this manifestation of jealousy of her sister which was an agreeable thing, anyway, for it implied a real depth of regard for him; but he was perturbed, for he did not know what Kate had told this sister of their last strange meeting.

He saluted her again, exclaiming:

'Never mind her. This our outing, isn't it?'

'I don't like her,' Ianthe added naïvely, 'she is so awfully fond of you.'

'Oh, confound her,' he cried; and then: 'You mustn't mind me saying that so, so sharply; you don't mind, do you?'

Ianthe's lips were soft and sweet. Sisters were quite unscrupulous. Masterman had heard of such cases before, but he had tenderness and a reluctance to wound anybody's susceptibility, let alone the feelings of a woman who loved. He was an artist not only in paint but in sentiment, and it is possible that he excelled in the less tangible medium.

'It's a little awkward,' he ventured. Ianthe

didn't understand, she didn't understand that at all.

'The difficulty, you see,' he said, with the air of one handling whimsically a question of perplexity that yet yielded its amusement, 'is . . . is Kate.'

'Kate?' said Ianthe.

'She is so – so gone, so absolutely gone.'

'Gone?'

'Well, she's really, really in love, deeply, deeply,' looking away anywhere but at her sister's eyes.

'With Chris Halton, do you mean?'

'Ho, ho!' he laughed. 'Chris who? Lord, no! With me, with me, isn't she?'

'With you!'

But Ianthe was quite positive, even a little ironical, about that. 'She is not. She rather dislikes you, Mr. Prince Charming, so there! We speak of you sometimes at night, in bed – we sleep together. She knows what I think of you. But she's quite, well, she doesn't like you at all – she acts the heavy sister.'

'Oh!' said Masterman, groping as it were for some light in his darkness.

'She – what do you think? – she warns me against you,' Ianthe continued.

'Against me?'

'As if I care. Do you?'

'No, no! I don't care.'

They left the dark bank where they had been standing and walked along to the bridge. Half-way up its steps to the road he paused and asked: 'Then who is it that is so fond of me?'

'Oh, you know, you know.' Ianthe nestled blissfully in his arm again.

'No, but who is it? I may be making another howler. I thought you meant Kate; what did she warn you of, I mean against me?'

They were now in the streets again, walking towards the tram centre. The shops were dark-ened and closed, but the cinemas lavished their unwanted illuminations on the street. There were no hurrying people, there was just strolling ease; the policemen at corners were chatting to other policemen, now in private clothes. The brilliant trams rumbled and clanged and stopped, the saloons were full and musical.

'What did she warn you against?' he repeated.

'You,' chuckled Ianthe.

'But what about? What has she got against me?'

'Everything. You know. You know you do.' The archness of Ianthe was objectively baffling, but under it all he read the significance, its invitation.

He waited beside her for a tram, but when it came he pleaded a further engagement in the city and left her, rather crestfallen, to her journey. He had no other engagement, he only wanted to be alone to sort out the things she had dangled before his mind, so he boarded the next car and walked from the Tutsan terminus to his cottage. Both girls were fond of him, then – Ianthe's candour left him no room for doubt – and they were both lying to each other about him. Well, he didn't mind that, he lied himself whenever it was necessary or suited him. Not often, but when truth was inappropriate to a sensitive-minded man this was his protective colouring. Why after all should sympathetic mendacity be a monopoly of polite society?

'But it's also the trick of thieves and seducers,' he muttered to himself. 'I'm not a thief, no, I'm

not a thief. As for the other thing, well, what
is there against me? – nothing, nothing at all.'
But a strange voiceless sigh seemed to echo from
the trees along the dark road; he walked on
more rapidly.

Three women! There was no doubt either
about the third; Ianthe had thought of Julia, too,
just as Kate had. What a fate for a misogamist!
He felt like a mouse being taken for a ride in
a bath chair. He had an invincible prejudice
against marriage, not as an institution, but
because he was perfectly aware of his incapacity
for faithfulness. His emotions were deep but un-
prolonged, they were fickle. Love was love, but
marriage turned love into the stone of Sisyphus.
At the sound of the marriage bell – a passing
bell – earth at his feet would burst into flame and
the sky above would pour upon him an un-
quenching profusion of tears. Love was a fine
ennobling thing, but though he had the will to
love he knew beyond the possibility of doubt
that his capacity for love was a meandering
strengthless thing. Even his loyalty to Julia Tern
– and that had the strongest flavour of any such
emotion that had ever beset him, no matter how

brief its term – even that was a deviating zig-zag loyalty. For he wanted to go on being jolly and friendly with Ianthe if only Julia did not get to know. With Kate, too, that tender melancholy woman. She would be vastly unhappy. Who was this Christopher whom Ianthe fondly imagined her sister to favour? Whoever he was, poor devil, he would not thank D. M. for his intervention. But he would drop all this; however had he, of all men, come to be plumped so suddenly into a state of things for which he had shown so little fancy in the past? Julia would despise him, she would be sure to despise him, sure to; and yet if he could only believe she would not it would be pleasant to go on being friendly with Ianthe pending . . . pending what?

Masterman was a very pliant man; but as things shaped themselves for him he did not go a step further with Ianthe, and it was not to Julia at all that he made love.

3

The armour, if it may be described as such, of

David Masterman and Kate Forrest took a course that was devoid of ecstasy, whatever other qualities may have illuminated their desires. It was an affair in which the human intentions, which are intellectual, were on both sides strong enough to subdue the efforts of passion, which are instinctive, to rid itself of the customary curbs, and to turn the clash of inhibitions, wherein the man proposes and the woman rejects, into a conflict not of ideal but of mere propriety. They were like two negative atoms swinging in a medium from which the positive flux was withdrawn; for them the nebulæ did not 'cohere into an orb.'

Kate's fine figure was not so fine as Julia Tern's; her dusky charms were excelled by those of Ianthe; but her melancholy immobility, superficial as it was, had a suggestive emotional appeal that won Masterman away from her rivals. Those sad eyes had but to rest on his and their depths submerged him. Her black hair had no special luxuriance, her stature no unusual grace; the eyes were almost blue and the thin oval face had always the flush of fine weather in it; but her strong hands, though not as white as

snow, were paler than milk, their pallor was
unnatural. Almost without an effort she drew
him away from the entangling Ianthe, and even
the image of Julia became but a fair cloud seen
in moonlight, delicate and desirable but very far
away; it would never return. Julia had observed
the relations between them – no discerning eye
could misread Kate's passion – and she gave up
her class, a secession that had a deep significance
for him, and a grief that he could not conceal
from Kate though she was too wise to speak
of it.

But in spite of her poignant aspect – for it
was in that appearance she made such a powerful appeal to Masterman; the way she would
wait silently for him on the outside of a crowd
of the laughing, chattering students was touching – she was an egotist of extraordinary type.
She believed in herself and in her virtue more
strongly than she believed in him or their mutual
love. By midsummer, after months of wooing,
she knew that the man who so passionately
moved her and whose own love she no less
powerfully engaged was a man who would
never marry, who had a morbid preposterous

horror of the domesticity and devotion that was her conception of living bliss. 'The hand that rocks the cradle rocks the world,' he said. He, too, knew that the adored woman, for her part, could not dream of a concession beyond the limits her virginal modesty prescribed. He had argued and stormed, sworn that baffled love turns irrevocably to hatred. She did not believe him, she even smiled, but he had behaved grossly towards her, terrified her, and they parted in anger.

He did not see her for many weeks. He was surprised and dismayed, his misery was profound. He knew he had loved her; he had not doubted its sincerity, but he had doubted its depth. Then one September evening she had come back to the class and afterwards she had walked along the road with him towards his home.

'Come to my house,' he said, 'you have never been to see it.'

She shook her head. It was getting dark and they walked on past his home further into the country. The eve was late, but it had come suddenly without the deliberation of sunset or the tenuity of dusk. Each tree was a hatful of the arriving blackness. They stood by a white gate under an elm, but they had little to say to each other.

'Come to my house,' he urged again and again. She shook her head. He was indignant at her distrust of him. Perhaps she was right, but he would never forgive her. The sky was now darker than the road; the sighing air was warm, with drifting spots of rain.

'Tell me,' she suddenly said, taking his arm, 'has anybody else ever loved you like that?'

He prevaricated: 'Like what?' He waited a long time for her answer. She gave it steadily. 'Like you want me to love you.'

He, too, hesitated. He kissed her. He wanted to tell her it was not wise to pry.

'Tell me,' she urged, 'tell me.'

'Yes,' he replied. He could not see her plainly in the darkness, but he knew of the tears that fell from her eyes.

'How unreasonable!' he thought, 'how stupid!' He began to tell the truth to her, about his feelings towards her, and towards those others, and about themselves – the truth as he conceived it.

She was almost alarmed, certainly shocked.

'But you don't believe such things,' she almost shivered, 'I'm sure you don't, it isn't right, it is not true.'

'It may not be true,' he declared implacably, 'but I believe it. The real warrant for holding a belief is not that it is true but that it satisfies you.'

She did not seem to understand that; she only answered irrelevantly, 'I'll make it up to you some day. I shall not change, David, towards you. We have got all our lives before us. I shan't alter, will you?'

'Not alter!' he began angrily, but then subduedly added, with a grim irony that she did not gather in; 'No, I shall not alter.' She leaned upon his breast murmuring: 'I'll make it all up to you, some day.'

He felt like a sick-minded man and was glad when they parted. He went back to his cottage grumbling audibly to himself. Why could he not take this woman with the loving and constant heart and wed her? He did not know why, but he knew he never would do that. She was fine to look upon, but she had ideas (if you could call them ideas) which he disliked. Her instincts and propensities were all wrong, they were antagonistic to him, just as, he felt, his were antagonistic to her. What was true, though, was her sorrow at what she called their misunderstandings; and what was profound, what was almost convincing, was her assumption (which but measured her own love for him) that he could not cease to love *her*. How vain that was. He had not loved any woman in the form she thought all love must take. These were not misunderstandings, they were just simply at opposite ends of a tilted beam; he the sophisticated, and she the innocent beyond the reach of his sophistries. But, good lord! what did it all matter? What did anything matter? He would not see her again. He undressed, and got into bed. He thought of Julia, of Ianthe, of Kate. . . . He had a dream in which he lay in a shroud upon a white board and was interrogated by a saint who carried a reporter's notebook and a fountain pen.

'What is your desire, sick-minded man?' the saint interrogated him, 'what consummation would exalt your languid eyes?'

'I want the present not to be. It is neither grave nor noble.'

'Then that *is* your sickness. That mere negation is at once your hope and end.'

'I do not know.'

'If the present so derides the dignified past surely your desire lies in a future incarnating beautiful old historic dreams?'

'I do not know.'

'Ideals are not in the past. They do not exist in any future. They rush on, and away, beyond your immediate activities, beyond the horizons that are for ever fixed, forever charging down upon us.'

'I do not know.'

'What is it you do know?' asked the exasperated saint, jerking his fountain pen to loosen its flow, and Masterman replied like a lunatic:

'I know that sealing wax is a pure and beautiful material, and you get such a lot of it for a penny.'

He woke and could not sleep again. He cursed Kate, he jeered at Julia, he anathematised Ianthe, until the bright eye of morning began to gild once more their broken images.

4

For a time the breach between them could not be healed, and during its interregnum he began to meet Ianthe again. But her eager devotion had lost its savour now, and he was conscious of his own mere amorous predacity, of treason to the dumb but benignant Kate, the sad-visaged woman whose chilly regard had riveted him, whose reproach, unspoken and indeed unseen, hovered almost annoyingly in his imagination.

Ianthe behaved evilly to Kate when she discovered that mutual infatuation for their one lover. Echoes of the sisters' feud, at first dim, but soon crashingly clear, reached him, touched him, moved him on Kate's behalf; all his loyalty belonged to her. What did it matter that he could not fathom his desire for her, or that Ianthe was his for a word, or that Kate's implacable virtue still offered its deprecatory hand, when Kate herself came back to him?

Kate was devout in the perfunctory way that denotes no apprehension of the mystery of sublime recognitions but is yet an effectual moral breakwater; she could be neither saint nor sinner. But her mind held fast to its promise : she would make it up, she would make it all up some day : and she did not feel or know that this was as much a promise to herself as to the man she loved.

They were to spend a picnic day together and she went to him for breakfast. Her tremors of propriety were fully exercised as she cycled along to his home; she was too fond of him and he was more than fond of her. But all her qualms were lulled, he did not appear in any of the half-anticipated *negligé,* he was beautifully and amusingly at home.

'My dear!' he exclaimed in the enjoyment of her presence; she stood staring at him as she removed her wrap, the morn though bright being fresh and cool : 'Why do I never do you justice! Why do I half forget! You are marvellously, irresistibly lovely. How do you do it – or how do I fail so?'

She could only answer him with blushes. His bungalow had but two rooms, both on the ground floor, one a studio and the other his living and sleeping-room. It was new, built of bricks and unpainted boards. The interior walls were un-plastered and undecorated except for three small saucepans hung on hooks, a shelf of dusty volumes, and nails, large rusty nails projecting everywhere, one holding a discarded collar and a clothes brush. A tall flat cupboard contained a narrow bed to be lowered for sleeping; huge portmanteaux and holdalls reposed in a corner beside a bureau; there was a big brass candle-pan on a chair beside the round stove. While he prepared breakfast the girl walked about the room, making shy replies to his hilarious questions. It was warm in there, but to her tidy comfort-loving heart the room was disordered and bare. She stood looking out of the window; the April air was bright but chilly, the grass in thin tufts fluttered and shivered.

'It is very nice,' she said to him once, 'but it's strange, and I feel that I ought not to be here.'

'Oh, never mind where you ought to be,' he cried, pouring out the coffee, 'that's where you are, you suit the place, you brighten and adorn it, it's your native setting, Kate. No – I know exactly what is running in your mind, you are going to ask if I suffer loneliness here. Well, I don't. A great art in life is the capacity to extract a flavour from something not obviously flavoured, but here it is all flavour. Come and look at things.'

He rose and led her from egg and toast to the world outside. Long fields of pasture and thicket followed a stream that followed other meadows, soon hidden by the ambulating many-folding valleys, and so on to the sea, a hundred miles away. Into his open door were blown, in their season, balls of thistledown, crisp leaves, twigs and dried grass, the reminder, the faint brush, of decay. Airs of wandering winds came in, odours of herbs, the fragrance of viewless flowers. The land in some directions was now being furrowed where corn was greenly to thrive, to wave in glimmering gold, to lie in the stook, to pile on giant stack. Horses were trailing a harrow across an upland below the park, the wind was flapping the coats of the drivers, the tails and manes of the horses, and heaving gladly in trees. A boy was firing some heaps of scutch grass and the smoke wore across the land in dense deliberate wreaths. Sportsmen's guns were sounding from the hollow park.

Kate followed Masterman around his cottage; he seemed to be fascinated by the smoke, the wind, the horses and men.

'Breakfast will be cold.'

How queerly he looked at her before he said: 'Yes, of course, breakfast will be getting cold,' and then added, inconsequently: 'Flowers are like men and women, they either stare brazenly at the sun or they bend humbly before it: but even the most modest desire the sun.'

When he spoke like that she always felt that the words held a half-hidden, perhaps libidinous, meaning, which she could not understand but only guess at; and she was afraid of her guesses. Full of curious, not to say absurd, superstitions about herself and about him, his strange oblique emotions startled her virginal understanding; her desire was to be good, very very good, but to be that she could not but suspect the impulses of most other people, especially the impulses of men. Well, perhaps she was right: the woman who hasn't any doubts must have many illusions.

He carried a bag of lunch and they walked out into the day. Soon the wind ceased, the brightness grew warm, the warmth was coloured; clouds lolled in the air like tufts of lilac. At the edge of a spinney they sat down under a tree. Boughs of wood blown down by the winter gales were now being hidden by the spring grass. A rabbit twenty yards away sat up and watched the couple, a fat grey creature. 'Hoi!' cried Kate, and the rabbit hopped away. It could not run very fast, it did not seem much afraid.

'Is it wounded?' she asked.

'No, I think it is a tame one, escaped from a farm or a cottage near us, I expect.'

Kate crept after it on hands and knees and it let her approach. She offered it the core of an apple she had just eaten. The rabbit took it and bit her finger. Then Kate caught it by the ears. It squealed but Kate held it to her bosom with delight, and the rabbit soon rested there, if not with delight at least with ease. It was warm against her breast. It was delicious to feel it there, to pull its ears and caress its fat flank, but as she was doing this she suddenly saw that its coat was infested with fleas. She dropped the rabbit with a scream of disgust and it rushed into the thicket.

'Come here,' said Masterman to her, 'let me search you; this is distressing.'

She knelt down before him and in spite of her wriggling he reassured her. 'It's rather a nice blouse,' he said.

'I don't care for it. I shall not wear it again. I shall sell it to someone or give it to them.'

'I would love to take it from you. . . .'

'You! Take it from me?'

'Yes, stitch by stitch.'

With an awkward movement of her arm she thrust at his face, crying loudly 'No, how dare you speak to me like that!'

'Is it very daring?' For a moment he saw her clenched hands, detestably bloodless, a symbol of roused virtue; but at once her anger was gone, Kate was contrite and tender. She touched his face with her white fingers softly as the settling of a moth. 'Oh, why did we come here?'

He did not respond to her caresses, he was sullen, they left the spinney; but as they walked she took his arm, murmuring:

'Forgive me, I'll make it all up to you, some day.'

Coyness and cunning, passion and pride, were

so much at odds that later on they quarrelled again. Kate knew that he would neither marry her nor let her go; she could neither let him go nor keep him. This figure of her distress amused him, he was callously provoking, and her resentment flared out at the touch of his scorn. With Kate there seemed to be no intermediate stages between docility and fury, or even between love and hatred.

'Why are you like this?' she cried, beating her pallid hands together, 'I have known you for so long.'

'Ah, we have known each other for so long, but as for really knowing you – no! I'm not a tame rabbit to be fondled any more.'

She stared for a moment, as if in recollection; then burst into ironical laughter. He caught her roughly in his arms but she beat him away.

'Oh, go to . . . go to. . . .'

'Hell?' he suggested.

'Yes,' she burst out tempestuously, 'and stop there.'

He was stunned by her unexpected violence. She was coarse, like Ianthe, after all. But he said steadily:

131

'I'm willing to go there, if you will only keep out of my way when I arrive.'

Then he left her standing in a lane: he hurried and ran, clambering over stiles and brushing through hedges, anything to get away from the detestable creature. She did not follow him and they were soon out of sight of each other. Anger and comminations swarmed to his lips, he branded her with frenzied opprobrium and all the beastliness that was in him. Nothing under heaven should ever pursuade him to approach the filthy beast again, the damned intolerable drab, never, never again, never.

But he came to a bridge. On it he rested. And in that bright air, that sylvan peace, his rancour fell away from him, like sand from a glass, leaving him dumb and blank at the meanness of his deed. He went back to the lane as fast as he could go. She was not there. 'Kate, Kate, my dove!' But he could not find her.

He was lost in the fields until he came at last upon a road and a lonely tavern thereby. It had a painted sign; a very smudgy fox, in an inexplicable attitude, destroying a fowl that looked like a plum-pudding but was intended to depict a snipe. At the stable door the tiniest black kitten in the world was shaping with timid belligerency at a young and fluffy goose who, ignoring it, went on sipping ecstatically from a pan of water. On the door were nailed, in two semi-circles of decoration, sixteen foxpads in various stages of decay, an entire spiral shaving from the hoof of a horse, and some chalk jottings:

2 *pads.*
3 *cruppers.*
1 *bellyband.*
2 *set britchin.*

The tavern was long and low and clean, its garden was bare but trim. There was comfort; he rested, had tea, and then in the bar his musings were broken upon by a ragged importunate old pedlar from Huddersfield.

'Born and bred in Slatterwick, it's no lie ah'm speaking, ah were born and bred Slatterwick, close to Arthur Brinkley's farm, his sister's in Canady, John Orkroyd took farm, Arthur's dead.'

'Humph!'

'And buried. That iron bridge at Jackamon's belongs to Daniel Cranmer. He's dead.'

'Humph!'

'And buried. From the iron bridge it's two miles and a quarter to Herbert Oddy's, that's the *Bay Horse,* am ah right, at Shelmersdyke. Three miles and three-quarters from Dyke to *Cock & Goat* at Shapley Fell, am ah right?'

Masterman, never having been within a hundred miles of Yorkshire, puffed at his cigarette, and nodded moodily, 'I suppose so' or 'Yes, yes.'

'From Arthur Brinkley's to th' iron bridge is one mile and a half and a bit, and from Arthur Brinkley's to Jury Cartright's is just four mile. He's dead, sir.'

'Yes.'

'And buried. Is that wrong? Am ah speaking wrong? No. It's a long step from yon, rough tramp for an old man.'

Masterman – after giving sixpence to the pedlar who, uttering a benediction, pressed upon him a card of shirt buttons – said 'Good evening,' and walked out to be alone upon the road with his once angry but now penitent mind. 'Kate, poor dear Kate!'

The sun was low down, lolling near the horizon, but there was an astonishing light upon the land. Cottage windows were blocks of solid gold in this lateral brilliance, shafts of shapely shade lay across leagues of fields, he could have counted every leaf among the rumpled boskage of the sycamores. A vast fan of indurated cloud, shell-like and pearly, was wavering over the western sky, but in the east were snowy and rounded masses like fabulous balloons. At a cross road he stood by an old sign post, its pillar plastered with the faded bill of a long ago circus. He could read every word of it but when he turned away he found everything had become dimmer. The wind arose, the forest began to roar like a heaving beast. All verdurous things leaned one way. A flock of starlings flew over him with one movement and settled on a rolling elm. How lonely it was. He took off his hat. His skull was fearfully tender – he had dabbed it too hard with his hairbrush that morning. His hair was growing thin, like his youth and his desires.

What had become of Kate, where had she hidden? What *would* be the end of it all? He would never see her again. He disliked everything about her, except herself. Her clothes, her speech, her walk, the way she carried her umbrella, her reticence that was nothing if not conspicuous, her melancholy, her angular concrete piety, her hands – in particular he disliked her pale hands. She had a mind that was cultivated as perfunctorily as a kitchen garden, with ideas like roots or beans, hostilities like briars, and a fence of prudery as tough as hoops of galvanised iron. And yet he loved her – or almost. He was ready to love her, he wanted to, he wanted her; her deep but guarded devotion – it was limited but it was devotion – compelled that return from him. It was a passionate return. He had tried to mould that devotion into a form that could delight him – he had failed. He knew her now, he could peer into her craven soul as one peers into an empty bottle, with one eye. For her the opportunities afforded by freedom were but the preludes to misadventure. What a fool she was!

When he reached home Kate stood in darkness at the doorway of his house. He exclaimed with delight, her surprising presence was the very centre of his desire; he wanted to embrace her, loving her deeply, inexplicably again, just in a moment.

'I want my bike,' the girl said sulkily. 'I left it inside this morning.'

'Ah, your bicycle! Yes, you did.' He unlocked the door. 'Wait, there should be a candle, there should be.'

She stood in the doorway until he had lit it.

'Come in, Kate,' he said, 'let me give you something. I think there is some milk, certainly I have some cake, come in, Kate, or do you drink beer, I have beer, come in, I'll make you something hot.'

But Kate only took her bicycle. 'I ought to have been home hours ago,' she said darkly, wheeling it outside and lighting the lantern. He watched her silently as she dabbed the wick; the pallor of her hands had never appeared so marked.

'Let's be kind to each other,' he said, detaining her, 'don't go, dear Kate.'

She pushed her bicycle out into the road.

'Won't you see me again?' he asked as she mounted it.

'I am always seeing you,' she called back, but her meaning was dark to him.

'Faugh! The devil! The fool!' He gurgled anathemas as he returned to his cottage. 'And me, too! What am I?'

But no mortal man could ever love a woman of that kind. She did not love him at all, had never loved him. Then what was it she did love? Not her virtue – you might as well be proud of the sole of your foot; it was some sort of pride, perhaps the test of her virtue that the conflict between them provoked, the contest itself alone alluring her, not its aim and end. She was never happier than when, having led him on, she thwarted him. But she would find that his metal was as tough as her own.

Before going to bed he spent an hour in writing very slowly a letter to Kate, telling her that he felt they would not meet again, that their notions of love were so unrelated, their standards so different. 'My morals are at least as high as yours, though likely you regard me

as a rip. Let us recognise then,' he wrote con-
cludingly, 'that we have come to the end of the
tether without once having put an ounce of strain
upon its delightful but very tense cord. But the
effort to keep the affair down to the level at
which you seem satisfied has wearied me. The
task of living down to that assures me that for
you the effort of living up to mine would be
consuming. I congratulate you, my dear, on
coming through scatheless, and that the only
appropriate condolences are my own – for myself.'

It was rather pompous, he thought, but then
she wouldn't notice that, let alone understand it.
She suffered not so much from an impediment
of speech – how could she when she spoke so
little? – as from an impediment of intellect,
which was worse, much worse, but not so noticeable, being so common a failing. She was, when
all was said and done, just a fool. It was a pity,
for bodily she must indeed be a treasure. What
a pity! But she had never had any love for him
at all, only compassion and pity for his bad
thoughts about her; he had neither pity for her
nor compunction – only love. Dear, dear, dear.

Blow out the candle. Lock the door. Good-night!

5

He did not see her again for a long time. He would have liked to have seen her, yes, just once more, but of course he was glad, quite glad, that she did not risk it and drag from dim depths the old passion to break again in those idiotic bubbles of propriety. She did not answer his letter – he was amused. Then her long silence vexed him, until vexation was merged in alarm. She had gone away from Tutsan – of course – gone away on family affairs – oh, naturally! – she might be gone away for ever. But a real grief came upon him. He had long mocked the girl, not only the girl but his own vision of her; now she was gone his mind elaborated her melancholy immobile figure into an image of beauty. Her absence, her silence, left him wretched. He heard of her from Ianthe, who renewed her blandishments; he was not unwilling to receive them now – he hoped their intercourse might be reported to Kate.

After many months he did receive a letter from her. It was a tender letter though ill-expressed, not very wise or informative, but he could feel that the old affection for him was still there, and he wrote her a long reply in which penitence and passion and appeal were mingled.

'I know now, yes, I see it all now; solutions are so easy when the proof of them is passed. We were cold to each other, it was stupid, I should have *made* you love me and it would have been well. I see it now. How stupid, how unlucky; it turned me to anger and you to sorrow. Now I can think only of you.'

She made no further sign, not immediately, and he grew dull again. His old disbelief in her returned. Bah! She loved him no more than a suicide loved the pond it dies in; she had used him for her senseless egoism, tempting him and fooling him, wantonly yes, wantonly; he had not begun it, and she took a chaste pride in saving herself from him. What was it the old writer had said? 'Chastity, by nature the gentlest of all affections – give it but its head – 'tis like a ramping and roaring lion.' Saving herself! Yes, she would save herself for marriage.

He even began to contemplate that outcome.

Her delayed letter, when it came, announced that she was coming home at once; he was to meet her train on the morning after the morrow.

It was a dull autumnal morning when he met her. Her appearance was not less charming than he had imagined it, though the charm was almost inarticulate and there were one or two crude touches that momentarily distressed him. But he met with a flush of emotion all her glances of gaiety and love that were somehow, vaguely, different—perhaps there was a shade less reserve. They went to lunch in the city and at the end of the meal he asked her:

'Well, why have you come back again?'

She looked at him intently: 'Guess!'

'I—well, no—perhaps—tell me, Kate, yourself.'

'You are different now, you look different, David.'

'Am I changed! Better or worse?'

She did not reply and he continued:

'You, too, are changed, I can't tell how it is, or where, but you are.'

'Oh, I am changed, much changed,' murmured Kate.

'Have you been well?'

'Yes.'

'And happy?'

'Yes.'

'Then how unwise of you to come back.'

'I have come back,' said Kate, 'to be happier. But somehow you are different.'

'You are different, too. Shall we ever be happy again?'

'Why – why not?' said Kate.

'Come on!' he cried hilariously, 'let us make a day of it. Come along!'

Out in the streets they wandered until rain began to fall. 'Come in here for a while.' They were passing a roomy dull building, the museum, and they went in together. It was a vast hollow-sounding flagstone place that had a central brightness fading into dim recesses and galleries of gloom. They examined a monster skeleton of something like an elephant, three stuffed apes and a picture of the dodo. Kate stood before them without interest or amusement, she just contemplated them. What did she want with an elephant, an ape, or a dodo! The glass exhibit cases were leaned upon by them, the pieces of coal neatly arranged and labelled, were stared at, beside the pieces of granite or coloured rock with long names ending in *orite, dorite* and *sorite* and so on to the precious gems including an imitation, as big as a bun, of a noted diamond. They leaned over them, repeating the names on the labels with the quintessence of vacuity. They hated it. There were beetles and worms of horror, butterflies of beauty, and birds that had been stuffed for so long that they seemed to be intoxicated; their beaks fitted them as loosely as a drunkard's hat, their glassy eyes were pathetically vague. After ascending a flight of stone steps David and Kate stooped for a long time over a case of sea-anemones that had been reproduced in gelatine by a German with a fancy for such things. From the railed balcony they could peer down into the well of the fusty-smelling museum. No one else was visiting it, they were alone with all things dead, things that had died millions of years ago and were yet simulating life. A footfall sounded so harsh in the corridors, boomed with such clangour, that they took slow diffident steps, almost tiptoeing, while Kate scarcely spoke at all and he conversed in murmurs. Whenever he coughed the whole place seemed to shudder. In the recess, hidden from prying eyes, David clasped her willing body in his arms. For once she was unshrinking and returned his fervour. The vastness, the emptiness, the deadness, worked upon their feelings with intense magic.

'Love me, David,' she murmured, and when they moved away from the gelatinous sea-urchins she kept both her arms clasped around him as they walked the length of the empty corridor. He could not perceive her intimations, their meaning was dark to him. She was so altered, this was another Kate.

'I have come home to make it all up to you,' she repeated, and he scarcely dared to understand her.

They approached a lecture room; the door was open, the room was empty, they went in and stood near the platform. The place was arranged like a tiny theatre, tiers of desks rising

145   K

in half circles on three sides, high up towards the ceiling. A small platform with a lecturer's desk confronted the rising tiers; on the wall behind it a large white sheet; a magic lantern on a pedestal was near and a blackboard on an easel. A pencil of white chalk lay broken on the floor. Behind the easel was a piano, with a duster on its lid. The room smelled of spilled acids. The lovers' steps upon the wooden floor echoed louder than ever after their peregrination upon the flagstones; they were timid of the sound and stood still, close together, silent. He touched her bosom and pressed her to his heart, but all her surrender seemed strange and nerveless. She was almost violently different; he had liked her old rejections, they were fiery and passionate. He scarce knew what to do, he understood her less than ever now. Dressed as she was in thick winter clothes it was like embracing a tree, it tired him. She lay in his arms waiting, waiting, until he felt almost stifled. Something like the smell of the acids came from her fur necklet. He was glad when she stood up, but she was looking at him intently. To cover his uneasiness he went to the blackboard and picking up a

146

piece of chalk he wrote the first inconsequent words that came into his mind. Kate stood where he had left her, staring at the board as he traced the words upon it: *We are but little children weak.*

Laughing softly she strolled towards him.

'What do you write that for? I know what it is.'

'What it is! – well, what is it?'

She took the chalk from his fingers.

'It's a hymn,' she went on, 'it goes . . . .'

'A hymn!' he cried, 'I did not know that.'

Underneath the one he had written she was now writing another line on the board: *Nor born to any high estate.*

'Of course,' he whispered, 'I remember it now. I sang it as a child – at – school – go on, go on.'

But she had thereupon suddenly turned away, silent, dropping her hands to her side. One of her old black moods had seized her. He let her go and picking up another fragment of chalk completed the verse:

What can we do for Jesu's sake
Who is so high and good and great?

147

She turned when he had finished and without a word walked loudly to the piano, fetched the duster and rubbed out the words they had written on the blackboard. She was glaring at him.

'How absurd you are' – he was annoyed – 'let us go out and get some tea.' He wandered off to the door, but she did not follow. He stood just outside gazing vacantly at a stuffed jay that had an indigo eye. He looked into the room again. She was there still just as he had left her; her head bent, her hands hanging clasped before her, the dimness covering and caressing her – a figure full of sad thoughts. He ran to her and crushed her in his arms again:

'Kate, my lovely.'

She was saying brokenly: 'You know what I said. I've come to make it all up to you. I promised, didn't I?'

Something shuddered in his very soul – too late, too late, this was no love for him. The magic lantern looked a stupid childish toy, the smell of the acid was repulsive. Of all they had written upon the blackboard one word dimly remained: *Jesu.*

148

She stirred in his arms. 'You are changed, David.'

'Changed, yes, everything is changed.'

'This is just like a theatre, like a play, as if we were acting.'

'Yes, as if we were acting. But we are not acting. Let us go up and sit in the gallery.'

They ascended the steps to the top ring of desks and looked down to the tiny platform and the white curtain. She sat fondling his hands, leaning against him.

Have you ever acted? – you would do it so well.'

'Why do you say that? Am I at all histrionic?'

'Does that mean insincere? Oh, no. But you are the person one expects to be able to do anything.'

'Nonsense! I've never acted. I suppose I could. It isn't difficult, you haven't to be clever, only courageous. I should think it very easy to be only an ordinary actor, but I'm wrong, no doubt. I thought it was easy to write – to write a play – until I tried. I once engaged myself to write a little play for some students to act. I had never done such a thing before and like other idiots I thought I hadn't ever done it simply because I hadn't ever wanted to. Heavens, how harassed I was and how ashamed! I could not do it. I got no further than the author's speech.'

'Well that was something. Tell me it.'

'It's nothing to do with the play. It's what the author says to the audience when the play is finished.'

She insisted on hearing it whatever it was. 'Oh, well,' he said at last. 'Let's do that properly, at least. I'll go down there and deliver it from the stage. You must pretend that you are the enthusiastic audience. Come and sit in the stalls.'

The went down together.

'Now imagine that this curtain goes up and I suddenly appear.'

Kate faintly clapped her hands. He stood upon the platform facing her, and taking off his hat, began:

'Ladies and Gentlemen,

'I am so deeply touched by the warmth of this reception, this utterly undeserved appreci-ation, that – forgive me – I have forgotten the

150

speech I had carefully prepared in anticipation
of it. Let me meet my obligation by telling
you a story; I think it is true, I made it up
myself. Once upon a time there was a poor
playwright – something like me – who wrote a
play – something like this – and at the end of
the performance the audience, a remarkably
handsome well-fed intellectual audience –
something like this – called him before the
curtain and demanded a speech. He protested
that he was unprepared and asked them to
allow him to tell them a story – something
like this. Well, that, too, was a remarkably
handsome well-fed intellectual audience, so
they didn't mind and he began again, Once
upon a time a poor playwright – and was just
about to repeat the story I have already twice
told you when suddenly, without a word of
warning, without a sound, without a compunction, the curtain swooped down and
chopped him clean in half.'

Masterman made an elaborate obeisance and
stepped off the platform.
'Is that all?' asked Kate.

'That's all.'

At that moment a loud bell clanged throughout the building signifying that the museum was about to close.

'Come along!' he cried, but Kate did not move, she still sat in the stalls.

'Don't leave me, David, I want to hear the play,' she said archly.

'There *was* no play and there *is* no play. Come, or we shall be locked in for the night.'

Still she sat on. He went to her and seized her hands.

'What does it matter!' she whispered, embracing him. 'I want to make it all up to you.'

He was astoundingly moved. She was marvellously changed. If she hadn't the beauty of perfection she had some of the perfection of beauty. He adored her.

'But no,' he said, 'it won't do, it really won't. Come, I have got to buy you something at once, a ring with a diamond in it, as big as a bun, an engagement ring, quickly, or the shops will be shut.'

He dragged the stammering bewildered girl away, down the stairs and into the street. The rain had ceased, the sunset sky was bright and Masterman was intensely happy.

A BROADSHEET BALLAD

A Broadsheet Ballad

*

At noon the tiler and the mason stepped down from the roof of the village church which they were repairing and crossed over the road to the tavern to eat their dinner. It had been a nice little morning but there were clouds massing in the south; Sam, the tiler, remarked that it looked like thunder. The two men sat in the dim little taproom eating, Bob, the mason, at the same time reading from a newspaper an account of a trial for murder.

'I dunno what thunder looks like,' Bob said, 'but I reckon this chap is going to be hung, though I can't rightly say for why. To my thinking he didn't do it at all; but murder's a bloody thing and someone ought to suffer for it.'

'I don't think,' spluttered Sam, as he impaled a flat piece of beetroot on the point of a pocket-knife and prepared to contemplate it with patience until his stuffed mouth was ready to receive it, 'he ought to be hung,'

CHAPTER SEVEN

A Broadsheet Ballad

*

AT noon the tiler and the mason stepped down from the roof of the village church which they were repairing and crossed over the road to the tavern to eat their dinner. It had been a nice little morning but there were clouds massing in the south; Sam, the tiler, remarked that it looked like thunder. The two men sat in the dim little taproom eating, Bob, the mason, at the same time reading from a newspaper an account of a trial for murder.

'I dunno what thunder looks like,' Bob said, 'but I reckon this chap is going to be hung, though I can't rightly say for why. To my thinking he didn't do it at all: but murder's a bloody thing and someone ought to suffer for it.'

'I don't think,' spluttered Sam, as he impaled a flat piece of beetroot on the point of a pocket-knife and prepared to contemplate it with patience until his stuffed mouth was ready to receive it, 'he ought to be hung.'

'There can be no other end for him though, with a mob of lawyers like that, and a jury too . . . why the rope's half round his neck this minute; he'll be in glory within a month; they only have three Sundays, you know, between the sentence and the execution. Well, hark at that rain then!'

A shower that began as a playful sprinkle grew to a powerful steady summer downpour. It splashed in the open window and the dim room grew more dim, and cool.

'Hanging's a dreadful thing,' continued Sam, 'and 'tis often unjust I've no doubt, I've no doubt at all.'

'Unjust! I tell you . . . at majority of trials those who give their evidence mostly knows nothing at all about the matter; them as knows a lot – they stays at home and don't budge, not likely!'

'No? But why?'

'Why? They has their reasons. I know that; I knows it for truth . . . hark at that rain, it's made the room feel cold.'

They watched the downfall in complete silence for some moments.

'Hanging's a dreadful thing,' Sam at length repeated, with almost a sigh.

'I can tell you a tale about that, Sam, in a minute,' said the other. He began to fill his pipe from Sam's brass box, which was labelled cough lozenges and smelled of paregoric.

'Just about ten years ago I was working over in Cotswold country. I remember I'd been into Gloucester one Saturday afternoon and it rained. I was jogging along home in a carrier's van; I never seen it rain like that afore, no, nor never afterwards, not like that. Br . . r . . r . .! it came down . . . bashing! And we came to a cross-roads where there's a public-house called *The Wheel of Fortune*, very lonely and un-sheltered it is just there. I seed a young woman standing in the porch awaiting us, but the carrier was wet and tired and angry or something and wouldn't stop. "No room" – he bawled out to her – "full up, can't take you!" and he drove on. "For the love o' God, mate," – I says – "pull up and take that young creature! She's . . . she's . . . can't you see!" "But I'm all behind as 'tis," he shouts to me, "you knows your gospel, don't you: time and tide wait for no man?"

"Ah, but dammit all, they always call for a feller," I says. With that he turned round and we drove back for the girl. She clumb in and sat on my knees; I squat on a tub of vinegar, there was nowhere else and I was right and all, she was going on for a birth. Well, the old van rattled away for six or seven miles; whenever it stopped you could hear the rain clattering on the tarpolin, or sounding outside on the grass as if it was breathing hard, and the old horse steamed and shivered with it. I had knowed the girl once in a friendly way, a pretty young creature, but now she was white and sorrowful and wouldn't say much. By and bye we came to another cross-roads near a village, and she got out there. "Good-day, my gal," I says, affable like, and; "Thank you, sir," says she, and off she popped in the rain with her umbrella up. A rare pretty girl, quite young, I'd met her before, a girl you could get uncommon fond of, you know, but I didn't meet her afterwards: she was mixed up in a bad business. It all happened in the next six months while I was working round those parts. Everybody knew of it. This girl's name was Edith and she had a younger sister

Agnes. Their father was old Harry Mallerton, kept *The British Oak* at North Quainy; he stuttered. Well, this Edith had a love affair with a young chap William, and having a very loving nature she behaved foolish. Then she couldn't bring the chap up to the scratch nohow by herself, and of course she was afraid to tell her mother or father: you know how girls are after being so pesky natural, they fear, oh, they do fear! But soon it couldn't be hidden any longer as she was living at home with them all, so she wrote a letter to her mother. "Dear Mother," she wrote, and told her all about her trouble.

'By all accounts the mother was angry as an old lion, but Harry took it calm like and sent for young William, who'd not come at first. He lived close by in the village, so they went down at last and fetched him.

'"All right, yes," he said, "I'll do what's lawful to be done. There you are, I can't say no fairer, that I can't."

'"No," they said, "you can't."

'So he kissed the girl and off he went, promising to call in and settle affairs in a day or two. The next day Agnes, which was the younger girl, she also wrote a note to her mother telling her some more strange news.

' "God above!" the mother cried out, "can it be true, both of you girls, my own daughters, and by the same man! Oh, whatever were you thinking on, both of ye! Whatever can be done now!" '

'What!' ejaculated Sam, 'both on 'em, both on 'em!'

'As true as God's my mercy – both on 'em – same chap. Ah! Mrs. Mallerton was afraid to tell her husband at first, for old Harry was the devil born again when he were roused up, so she sent for young William herself, who'd not come again, of course, not likely. But they made him come, oh, yes, when they told the girls' father.

' "Well, may I go to my d . . d . . d . . damnation at once!" roared old Harry – he stuttered you know – "at once, if that ain't a good one!" So he took off his coat, he took up a stick, he walked down street to William and cut him off his legs. Then he beat him till he howled for his mercy, but you couldn't stop old Harry once he were roused up – he was the devil born again. They do say as he beat him for a solid hour; I can't say as to that, but then old Harry picked him up and carried him off to *The British Oak* on his own back, and threw him down in his own kitchen between his own two girls like a dead dog. They do say that the little one, Agnes, flew at her father like a raging cat until he knocked her senseless with a clout over head; rough man he was.'

'Well, a' called for it sure,' commented Sam.

'Her did,' agreed Bob, 'but she was the quietest known girl for miles round those parts, very shy and quiet.'

'A shady lane breeds mud,' said Sam.

'What do you say? – Oh, ah! – mud, yes. But pretty girls both, girls you could get very fond of, skin like apple bloom, and as like as two pinks they were. They had to decide which of them William was to marry.'

'Of course, ah!'

' "I'll marry Agnes," says he.'

' "You'll not," says the old man, "you'll marry Edie." '

' "No, I won't," William says, "it's Agnes I love and I'll be married to her or I won't be married to e'er of 'em." All the time Edith sat

163

quiet, dumb as a shovel, never a word, crying a bit; but they do say the young one went on like a . . . a young . . . Jew.'

'The Jezebel!' commented Sam.

'You may say it; but wait, my man, just wait. Another cup of beer? We can't go back to church until this humbugging rain have stopped.'

'No, that we can't.'

'It's my belief the 'bugging rain won't stop this side of four o'clock.'

'And if the roof don't hold it off it 'ull spoil they Lord's Commandments that's just done up on the chancel front.'

'Oh, they be dry by now.' Bob spoke reassuringly and then continued his tale. ' "I'll marry Agnes or I won't marry nobody," William says, and they couldn't budge him. No, old Harry cracked on but he wouldn't have it, and at last Harry says: "It's like this." He pulls a half-crown out of his pocket and, "heads it's Agnes," he says, "or tails it's Edith," he says.'

'Never! Ha! ha!' cried Sam.

'Heads it's Agnes, tails it's Edie, so help me God. And it come down Agnes, yes, heads it was -- Agnes -- and so there they were.'

164

'And they lived happy ever after?'

'Happy! You don't know your human nature, Sam; where ever was you brought up? "Heads it's Agnes," said old Harry, and at that Agnes flung her arms round William's neck and was for going off with him then and there; ha! but this is how it happened about that. William hadn't any kindred, he was a lodger in the village, and his landlady wouldn't have him in her house one mortal hour when she heard all of it; give him the rightabout there and then. He couldn't get lodgings anywhere else, nobody would have anything to do with him. So, of course, for safety's sake, old Harry had to take him, and there they all lived together at *The British Oak* – all in one happy family. But the girls couldn't bide the sight of each other, so their father cleaned up an old out-house in his yard that was used for carts and hens and put William and his Agnes out in it. And there they had to bide. They had a couple of chairs, a sofa, and a bed and that kind of thing, and the young one made it quite snug.'

' 'Twas a hard thing for that other, that Edie, Bob.'

'It was hard, Sam, in a way, and all this was

165

happening just afore I met her in the carrier's van. She was very sad and solemn then; a pretty girl, one you could like. Ah, you may choke me, but there they lived together. Edie never opened her lips to either of them again, and her father sided with her, too. What was worse, it came out after the marriage that Agnes was quite free of trouble – it was only a trumped-up game between her and this William because he fancied her better than the other one. And they never had no child, them two, though when poor Edie's mischance come along I be damned if Agnes weren't fonder of it than its own mother, a jolly sight more fonder, and William – he fair worshipped it.'

'You don't say!'

'I do. 'Twas a rum go, that, and Agnes worshipped it, a fact, can prove it by scores of people to this day, scores, in them parts. William and Agnes worshipped it, and Edie – she just looked on, long of it all, in the same house with them, though she never opened her lips again to her young sister to the day of her death.'

'Ah, she died? Well, it's the only way out of such a tangle, poor woman.'

'You're sympathising with the wrong party.' Bob filled his pipe again from the brass box; he ignited it with deliberation; going to the open window he spat into a puddle in the road. 'The wrong party, Sam; 'twas Agnes that died. She was found on the sofa one morning stone dead, dead as a adder.'

'God bless me,' murmured Sam.

'Poisoned,' added Bob, puffing serenely.

'Poisoned!'

Bob repeated the word 'poisoned.' 'This was the way of it,' he continued; 'one morning the mother went out in the yard to collect her eggs, and she began calling out: "Edie, Edie, here a minute, come and look where that hen have laid her egg; I would never have believed it," she says. And when Edie went out her mother led her round the back of the out-house, and there on the top of a wall this hen had laid an egg. "I would never have believed it, Edie," she says, "scooped out a nest there beautiful, ain't she; I wondered where her was laying. T'other morning the dog brought an egg round in his mouth and laid it on the doormat. There now, Aggie, Aggie, here a minute, come and look where the hen have laid that egg." And as Aggie didn't answer the mother went in and found her on the sofa in the out-house, stone dead.

'How'd they account for it?' asked Sam, after a brief interval.

'That's what brings me to the point about this young feller that's going to be hung,' said Bob, tapping the newspaper that lay upon the bench. 'I don't know what would lie between two young·women in a wrangle of that sort; some would get over it quick, but some would never sleep soundly any more not for a minute of their mortal lives. Edie must have been one of that sort. There's people living there now as could tell a lot if they'd a mind to it. Some knowed all about it; could tell you the very shop where Edith managed to get hold of the poison, and could describe to me or to you just how she administrated it in a glass of barley water. Old Harry knew all about it, he knew all about everything, but he favoured Edith and he never budged a word. Clever old chap was Harry, and nothing came out against Edie at the inquest – nor the trial neither.'

'Was there a trial then?'

'There was a kind of a trial. Naturally. A beautiful trial. The police came and fetched poor William, they took him away and in due course he was hanged.'

'William! But what had he got to do with it?'

'Nothing. It was rough on him, but he hadn't played straight, and so nobody struck up for him. They made out a case against him—there was some unlucky bit of evidence which I'll take my oath old Harry knew something about—and William was done for. Ah, when things take a turn against you it's as certain as twelve o'clock, when they take a turn; you get no more chance than a rabbit from a weasel. It's like dropping your matches into a stream, you needn't waste the bending of your back to pick them out— they're no good on, they'll never strike again. And Edith, she sat in court through it all, very white and trembling and sorrowful, but when the judge put his black cap on they do say she blushed and looked across at William and gave a bit of a smile. Well, she had to suffer for his doings, so why shouldn't he suffer for hers? That's how I look at it. . . .'

'But God-a-mighty . . .!'

'Yes, God-a-mighty knows. Pretty girls they were, both, and as like as two pinks.'

There was quiet for some moments while the tiler and the mason emptied their cups of beer. 'I think,' said Sam then, 'the rain's give over now.'

'Ah, that it has,' cried Bob. 'Let's go and do a bit more on this 'bugging church or she won't be done afore Christmas.'

COTTON

CHAPTER EIGHT

Cotton

*

AT the place where the road from Carnaby Down ends in the main western highway that goes towards Bath there stands, or once stood, a strongly built stone cottage confronting, on the opposite side of the high road, a large barn and some cattle stalls. A man named Cotton lived with his wife lonely in this place, their whole horizon bounded by the hedges and fences of their farm. His Christian name, for some unchristian reason, was Janifex; people called him Jan, possibly because it rhymed with his wife's name, which was Ann. And Ann was a robust managing woman of five-and-thirty, childless, full of desolating cleanliness and kindly tyrannies, with no perceptions that were not determined by her domestic ambition, and no sympathies that could interfere with her diurnal energies whatever they might be. Jan was a mild husbandman, prematurely aged, with large teeth and since 'forty winters had besieged his brow,' but little hair. Sometimes one of the large teeth would drop out, leaving terrible gaps when he opened his mouth, and turning his patient smile to a hideous leer. These evacuations, which were never restored, began with the death of Queen Victoria; throughout the reign of her successor great events were punctuated by similar losses, until at last Jan could masticate, in his staid old manner, only in one overworked corner of his mouth.

He would rise of a morning throughout the moving year at five of the clock; having eaten his bread and drunk a mug of cocoa he would don a long white jacket and cross the road diagonally to the gate at the eastern corner of the sheds. These were capped by the bright figure of a golden cockerel, voiceless but useful, flaunting always to meet the challenge of the wind. Sometimes in his deliberate way Jan would lift his forlorn eyes in the direction of the road coming from the east, but he never turned to the other direction, as that would have cost him a physical effort, and bodily flexion had ceased years and years ago. Do roads ever run backward — leaps not forward the eye? As he unloosed the gate of the yard his great dog would lift its chained head from some sacks under a cart, and a peacock would stalk out from the belt of pines that partly encircled the buildings. The man would greet them, saying, 'Oh, ah!' In the rick-yard he would pause to release the fowls from their hut and watch them run to the stubbles or spurn the chaff with their claws as they ranged between the stacks. If the day were windy the chaff would fall back in clouds upon their bustling feathers, and that delighted his simple mind. It is difficult to account for his joy in this thing, for though his heart was empty of cruelty it seemed to be empty of everything else. Then he would pass into the stalls and with a rattle of can and churn the labour of the day was begun.

Thus he lived, with no temptations, and few desires except perhaps for milk puddings, which for some reason concealed in Ann's thrifty bosom he was only occasionally permitted to enjoy. Whenever his wife thought kindly of him she would give him a piece of silver and he would traipse a mile in the evening, a mile along to the *Huntsman's Cup,* and take a tankard of beer. On his return he would tell Ann of the things he had seen, the people he had met, and other events of his journey.

Once, in the time of spring, when buds were bursting along the hedge coverts and birds of harmony and swiftness had begun to roost in the wood, a blue-chinned Spaniard came to lodge at the farm for a few weeks. He was a labourer working at some particular contract upon the estate adjoining the Cottons' holding, and he was accommodated with a bed and an abundance of room in a clean loft behind the house. With curious shoes upon his feet, blazing check trousers tightly fitting upon his thighs, a wrapper of pink silk around his neck, he was an astonishing figure in that withdrawn corner of the world. When the season chilled him a long black cloak with a hood for his head added a further strangeness. Juan da Costa was his name. He was slightly round-shouldered with an uncongenial squint in his eyes; though he used but few words of English his ways were beguiling. He sang very blithely shrill Spanish songs, and had a pleasant courtesy of manner that presented a deal of attraction to the couple, particularly Ann, whose casual heart he reduced in a few hours to

kindness, and in a few days, inexplicably perhaps, to a still warmer emotion – yes, even in the
dull blankness of that mind some ghostly star
could glimmer. From the hour of his arrival she
was an altered woman, although, with primitive
subtlety, the transition from passivity to passion
was revealed only by one curious sign, and that
was the spirit of her kindness evoked for the
amiable Jan, who now fared mightily upon his
favourite dishes.

Sometimes the Spaniard would follow Jan
about the farm. 'Grande!' he would say, gestur-
ing with his arm to indicate the wide-rolling hills.

'Oh, ah!' Jan would reply, 'there's a heap o'
land in the open air.'

The Spaniard does not understand! He asks:
'What?'

'Oh, ah!' Jan would echo.

But it was the cleanly buxom Ann to whom
Da Costa devoted himself. He brought home
daily, though not ostensibly to her, a bunch of
the primroses, a stick of snowbudded sallow, or
a sprig of hazel hung with catkins, soft caressable
things. He would hold the hazel up before Ann's
uncomprehending gaze and strike the lemon-

coloured powder from the catkins on to the expectant adjacent buds, minute things with stiff female prongs, red like the eyes of the white rabbit which Ann kept in the orchard hutch.

One day Juan came home unexpectedly in mid-afternoon. It was a cold dry day and he wore his black cloak and hood.

'See,' he cried, walking up to Ann, who greeted him with a smile; he held out to her a posy of white violets tied up with some blades of thick grass. She smelt them but said nothing. He pressed the violets to his lips and again held them out, this time to her lips. She took them from him and tucked them into the front of her bodice while he watched her with delighted eyes.

'You . . . give . . . me . . . somethin' . . . for . . . *los flores?*'

'Piece a cake!' said Ann, moving towards the pantry door.

'Ah . . . cake!'

As she pulled open the door, still keeping a demure eye upon him, the violets fell out and down upon the floor, unseen by her. He rushed towards them with a cry of pain and a torrent of his strange language; picking them up he followed her into the pantry, a narrow place almost surrounded by shelves with pots of pickles and jam, plates, cups and jugs, a scrap of meat upon a trencher, a white bowl with cob nuts and a pair of iron crackers.

'See . . . lost!' he cried shrilly as she turned to him. She was about to take them again when he stayed her with a whimsical gesture.

'Me . . . me,' he said, and brushing her eyes with their soft perfume he unfastened the top button of her bodice while the woman stood motionless; then the second button, then the third. He turned the corners inwards and tucked the flowers between her flesh and underlinen. They stood eyeing one another, breathing uneasily, but with a pretence at nonchalance. 'Ah!' he said suddenly; before she could stop him he had seized a few nuts from the white bowl and holding open her bodice where the flowers rested he dropped the nuts into her warm bosom. 'One . . . two . . . three!'

'Oh . . . !' screamed Ann mirthfully, shrinking from their tickling, but immediately she checked her laughter – she heard footsteps.

Beating down the grasping arms of the Spaniard she darted out of the doorway and shut him in the pantry, just in time to meet Jan coming into the kitchen and bawling for a chain he required.

'What d'ye want?' said Ann.

'That chain for the well-head, gal, it's hanging in the pantry.' He moved to the door.

''Taint,' said Ann barring his way. 'It's in the barn, I took it there yesterday, on the oats it is, you'll find it, I took it over yesterday. Clear off with your dirty boots.' She 'hooshed' him off much as she 'hooshed' the hens out of the garden. Immediately he was gone she pulled open the pantry door and was confronted by the Spaniard holding a long clasp knife in his raised hand. On seeing her he just smiled, threw down the knife and took the bewildered woman into his arms.

'Wait, wait,' she whispered, and breaking from him she seized a chain from a hook and ran out after her husband with it, holding up a finger of warning to the Spaniard as she brushed past him. She came back panting, having made some sort of explanation to Jan; entering the kitchen quietly she found the Spaniard's cloak lying upon the table; the door of the pantry was shut and he had apparently gone back there to await her. Ann moved on tiptoe round the tables; picking up the cloak she enveloped herself in it and pulled the hood over her head. Having glanced with caution through the front window to the farmyard, she coughed and shuffled her feet on the flags. The door of the pantry moved slowly open; the piercing ardour of his glance did not abash her, but her curious appearance in his cloak moved his shrill laughter. As he approached her she seized his wrists and drew him to the door that led into the orchard at the back of the house; she opened it and pushed him out, saying 'Go on, go on.' She then locked the door against him. He walked up and down outside the window, making lewd signs to her. He dared not call out for fear of attracting attention from the farmyard in front of the house. He stood still, shivered, pretended in dumb show that he was frozen. She stood at the window in front of him and nestled provocatively in his cloak. But when he put his lips against the pane he drew the gleam of her languishing eyes closer and closer to meet his kiss through the glass. Then she stood up, took off the black cloak, and putting her hand into her bosom brought out the three nuts, which she held up to him. She stood there fronting the Spaniard enticingly, dropped the nuts back into her bosom . . . one . . . two . . . three . . . and then went and opened the door.

In a few weeks the contract was finished, and one bright morning the Spaniard bade them each farewell. Neither of them knew, so much was their intercourse restricted, that he was about to depart, and Ann watched him with perplexity and unhappiness in her eyes.

'Ah, you Cotton, good-bye I say, and you *señora,* I say good-bye.' With a deep bow he kissed the rough hand of the blushing countrywoman. *'Bueno.'* He turned with his kit bag on his shoulder, waved them an airy hand and was gone.

On the following Sunday Jan returned from a visit in the evening and found the house empty. Ann was out, an unusual thing, for their habits were fixed and deliberate as the stars in the sky. The sunsetting light was lying in meek patches on the kitchen wall, turning the polished iron pans to the brightness of silver, reddening the string of onions, and filling glass jars with solid crystal. He had just sat down to remove his heavy boots when Ann came in, not at all the workaday Ann but dressed in her best clothes smelling of scent and swishing her stiff linen.

'Hullo,' said Jan, surprised at his wife's pink face and sparkling eyes, 'bin church?'

'Yes, church,' she replied, and sat down in her finery. Her husband ambled about the room for various purposes and did not notice her furtive dabbing of her eyes with her handkerchief. Tears from Ann were inconceivable.

The year moved through its seasons, the lattermath hay was duly mown, the corn stooked in rows; Ann was with child and the ridge of her stays was no longer visible behind her plump shoulders. Fruit dropped from the orchard boughs, the quince was gathered from the wall, the hunt swept over the field. Christmas came and went, and then a child was born to the Cottons, a dusky boy, who was shortly christened Juan.

'He was a kind chap, that man,' said Ann,

183

'and we've no relations to please, and it's like your name – and your name *is* outlandish!'

Jan's delight now was to sit and muse upon the child as he had ever mused upon chicken, lambs and calves. 'Oh, ah!' he would say, popping a great finger into the babe's mouth, 'Oh, ah!' But when, as occasionally happened, the babe squinted at him, a singular fancy would stir in his mind, only to slide away before it could congeal into the likeness of suspicion.

Snow, when it falls near spring on those Cotswold hills, falls deeply, and the lot of the husbandmen is hard. Sickness, when it comes, comes with a flail and in its hobnailed boots. Contagious and baffling, disease had stricken the district; in mid-March great numbers of the country folk were sick abed, hospitals were full, and doctors were harried from one dawn to another. Jan would come in of an evening and recite the calendar of the day's dooms gathered from men of the adjacent fields.

'Amos Green 'ave gone then, pore o' chap.'

'Pore Amos,' the pitying Ann would say, wrapping her babe more warmly.

'And Buttifant's coachman.'

'Dear, dear, what 'll us all come to?'

'Mrs. Jocelyn was worse 'en bad this morning.'

'Never Jan! Us'll miss 'er.'

'Ah, and they do say Parson Rudwent won't last out the night.'

'And whom's to bury us then?' asked Ann.

The invincible sickness came to the farm. Ann one morning was weary, sickly, and could not rise from her bed. Jan attended her in his clumsy way and kept coming in from the snow to give her comforts and food, but at eve she was in fever and lay helpless in the bed with the child at her breast. Jan went off for the doctor, not to the nearest village for he knew that quest to be hopeless, but to a tiny town high on the wolds two miles away. The moon, large, sharp and round, blazed in the sky, and its light sparkled upon the rolling fields of snow; his boots were covered at every muffled step; the wind sighed in the hedges and he shook himself for warmth. He came to the hill at last; half-way up was a church, its windows glowing with warm-looking light and its bells pealing cheerfully. He passed on and higher up met a priest trotting downwards in black cassock and saintly hat, his hands tucked into his wide sleeves, trotting to keep himself warm, and humming as he went. Jan asked a direction of the priest, who gave it with many circumstances of detail, and after they had parted he could hear the priest's voice call still further instructions after him as long as he was in sight. 'Oh, ah!' said Jan each time, turning and waving his hand. But after all his mission was a vain one; the doctor was out and away, it was improbable that he would be able to come, and the simple man turned and went home with a dull heart. When he reached the farm Ann was delirious but still clung to her dusky child, sleeping snugly at her bosom. The man sat up all night before the fire waiting vainly for the doctor, and the next day he himself became ill. And strangely enough as he worked among his beasts the crude suspicion in his mind about the child took shape and worked without resistance until he came to suspect and by easy degrees to apprehend fully the time and occasion of Ann's duplicity.

'Nasty filthy dirty thing!' he murmured from his sick mind. He was brushing the dried mud

from the hocks of an old bay horse, but it was
not of his horse he was thinking. Later he stood
in the rickyard and stared across the road at the
light in their bedroom. Throwing down the
fork with which he had been tossing beds of
straw he shook his fist at the window and
cried out: 'I hate 'er, I does, nasty filthy dirty
thing!'

When he went into the house he replenished
the fire, but found he could take no further care
for himself or the sick woman; he just stupidly
doffed his clothes and in utter misery and reck-
lessness stretched himself in the bed with Ann.
He lay for a long while with aching brows, a
snake-strangled feeling in every limb, an un-
quenchable drouth in his throat, and his wife's
body burning beside him. Outside the night was
bright, beautiful and still sparkling with frost;
quiet, as if the wind had been wedged tightly in
some far corner of the sky, except for a cracked
insulator on the telegraph pole just near the
window, that rattled and hummed with mon-
strous uncare. That, and the ticking of the
clock! The lighted candle fell from its sconce
on to the mantelpiece; he let it remain and it

flickered out. The glow from the coals was thick upon the ceiling and whitened the brown ware of the teapot on the untidy hearth. Falling asleep at last he began dreaming at once, so it seemed, of the shrill cry of lambs hailing him out of wild snow-covered valleys; so wild and prolonged were the cries that they woke him, and he knew himself to be very ill, very ill indeed. The child was wailing piteously, the room was in darkness, the fire out, but the man did not stir, he could not care, what could he do with that flame behind his eyes and the misery of death consuming him? But the child's cries were unceasing and moved even his numbed mind to some effort. 'Ann!' he gasped. The poor wife did not reply. 'Ann!' He put his hand out to nudge her; in one instant the blood froze in his veins and then boiled again. Ann was cold, her body hard as a wall, dead . . . dead. Stupor returned upon him; the child, unhelped, cried on, clasped to that frozen breast until the man again roused himself to effort. Putting his great hands across the dead wife he dragged the child from her arms into the warmth beside him, gasping as he did so 'Nasty . . . dirty . . . thing.'

It exhausted him, but the child was still unpaci-
fied and again he roused himself and felt for a
biscuit on the table beside the bed. He crushed
a piece in his mouth and putting the soft pap
upon his finger fed thus the hungry child until
it was stilled. By now the white counterpane
spread vast like a sea, heaving and rocking with
a million waves, the framework of the bedstead
moving like the tackle of tossed ships. He knew
there was only one way to stem that sickening
movement. 'I hate 'er, I does,' rose again upon
his lips, and drawing up his legs that were at
once chilly and streaming with sweat, full of his
new hatred he urged with all his might his wife's
cold body to the edge of the bed and withdrew
the bedclothes. Dead Ann toppled and slid from
him and her body clumped upon the floor with
a fall that shook the room; the candle fell from
the mantelpiece, bounced upon the teapot and
rolled stupidly along the bare boards under the
bed. 'Hate 'er!' groaned the man; he hung
swaying above the woman and tried to spit upon
her. He sank back again to the pillow and the
child, murmuring 'Oh, ah!' and gathering it
clumsily to his breast. He became tranquil then,

and the hollow-sounding clock beat a dull rhythm into his mind, until that sound faded out with all light and sound, and Jan fell into sleep and died, with the dusky child clasped in his hard dead arms.

POMONA'S BABE

Pomona's Babe

*

JOHNNY FLYNN was then seventeen years old. At that age you could not call him 'boy,' without vexing him, or 'man,' without causing him to blush - his teasing ruddy and uproarious mother delighted to produce either or both of these manifestations, for her offspring was a pale mild creature - but he had given a deal of thought to many manly questions. Marriage, for instance, was one of these. That was an institution he admired, but whose joys, whatever they were, he was not anxious to experience; its difficulties and disasters as ironically outlined by the widow Flynn were the subject of his grossest scepticism - scepticism in general being not the least prominent characteristic of Johnny Flynn.

Certainly his sister Pomona was not married; she was only sixteen, an age too early for such bliss; but all the same she was going to have a baby. He had quarrelled with his mother about most things; she delighted in quarrels, they amused her very much; but on this occasion she

CHAPTER NINE

Pomona's Babe

*

JOHNNY FLYNN was then seventeen years old. At that age you could not call him 'boy' without vexing him, or 'man' without causing him to blush – his teasing ruddy and uproarious mother delighted to produce either or both of these manifestations, for her offspring was a pale mild creature – but he had given a deal of thought to many manly questions. Marriage, for instance, was one of these. That was an institution he admired, but whose joys, whatever they were, he was not anxious to experience; its difficulties and disasters as ironically outlined by the widow Flynn were the subject of his grossest scepticism – scepticism in general being not the least prominent characteristic of Johnny Flynn.

Certainly his sister Pomona was not married; she was only sixteen, an age too early for such bliss; but all the same she was going to have a baby. He had quarrelled with his mother about most things; she delighted in quarrels, they amused her very much; but on this occasion she

193   N

was really very angry, or she pretended to be so
— which was worse, much worse than the real
thing.

The Flynns were poor people, quite poor,
living in two top-floor rooms at the house of a
shoemaker, also moderately poor, whose pelting
and hammering of soles at evening were a
durable grievance to Johnny. He was fond of
the shoemaker, a kind, bulky, tall man of fifty,
though he did not like the shoemaker's wife, as
bulky as her husband, and as tall, but not kind
to him or to anything except Johnny himself;
nor did he like any of the other lodgers, of
whom there were several, all without exception
beyond the reach of affluence. The Flynn apart-
ments afforded a bedroom in front for Mrs.
Flynn and Pomona, a room where Johnny
seldom intruded, never without a strained sense
of sanctity similar to the feeling he experienced
when entering an empty church, as he sometimes
did. He slept in the other room, the living room,
an arrangement that also annoyed him — he was
easily annoyed — for he could never go to bed
until mother and sister had retired, and for the
same reason he had always to rise before they got

up, an exasperating abuse of domestic privilege.

One night he had just slipped happily into his bed, and begun to read a book called *Rasselas,* which the odd-eyed man at the public library had commended to him, when his mother returned to the room, first tapping at the door, for Johnny was a prude, as she knew, not only from instinct and observation but from protests which had occasionally been addressed to her by the indignant boy. She came in now only half clad, in petticoat and stockinged feet, her arms were quite bare. They were powerful arms, as they had need to be, for she was an ironer of linen at a laundry, but they were nice to look at, and sometimes Johnny liked looking at them, though he did not care for her to run about like that very often. Mrs. Flynn sat down at the foot of his couch and stared at her son.

'Johnny,' she began steadily, but paused to rub her forehead with her thick white shiny fingers. 'I don't know how to tell you I'm sure, or what you'll say. . . .' Johnny shook *Rasselas* rather impatiently and heaved a protesting sigh. 'I can't think,' continued his mother, 'no, I can't think that it's our Pomony, but there she is, and it's got to be done—I must tell you; besides, you're the only man in our family now, so it's only right for you, you see, and she's going to have a baby—our Pomony!'

The boy turned his face to the wall, although his mother was not looking at him—she was staring at that hole in the carpet near the fender. At last he said 'Humph! . . . well?' And as his mother did not say anything, he added, 'What about it? I don't mind.' Mrs. Flynn was horrified at his unconcern, or she pretended to be so; Johnny was never sure about the genuineness of her moods. It was most unfilial, but he was like that—so was Mrs. Flynn. Now she cried out, 'You'll *have* to mind, there, you must. I can't take everything on my own shoulders. You're the only man left in our family now— you must, Johnny. What are we to do?'

He glared at the wallpaper a foot from his eyes. It had an unbearable pattern of blue but otherwise indescribable flowers; he had it in his mind to have some other pattern there—some day.

'Eh?' asked his mother sharply, striking the foot of the bed with her fist.

'Why . . . there's nothing to be done . . . now . . . I suppose.' He was blushing furiously. 'How did it happen – when will it be?'

'It's a man she knows. He got hold of her. His name is Stringer. Another two months about. Stringer. Hadn't you noticed anything? Everybody else has. You are a funny boy, can't make you out at all, Johnny, I can't make you out. Stringer his name is, but he shall pay dearly for it, and that's what I want you – to talk to you about. Of course, he denies everything; they always do.'

Mrs. Flynn sighed at this disgusting perfidy, brightening however when her son began to discuss the problem. But she talked so long, and he got so sleepy at last, that he was very glad when she went to bed again. Secretly she was both delighted and disappointed at his easy acceptance of her dreadful revelation; fearing a terrible outburst of anger, she had kept the knowledge from him for a long time. She was glad to escape that, it is true, but she rather hungered for some flashing reprobation of this unknown beast, this Stringer. She swore she would bring him to book, but she felt old and lonely, and Johnny was a strange son, not very virile. The mother had told Pomona terrifying prophetic tales of what Johnny would do, what he would be certain to do. He would, for instance, murder that Stringer and drive Pomony into the street; of course he would. Yet here he was, quite calm about it, as if he almost liked it. Well, she had told him, she could do no more, she would leave it to him.

In the morning Johnny greeted his sister with tender affection, and at evening, having sent her to bed, he and his mother resumed their discussion.

'Do you know, mother,' he said, 'she is quite handsome; I never noticed it before.'

Mrs. Flynn regarded him with desperation, and then informed him that his sister was an ugly, disgusting little trollop who ought to be birched.

'No, no, you are wrong, mother, it's bad, but it's all right.'

'You think you know more about such things than your own mother, I suppose.' Mrs. Flynn sniffed and glared.

He said it to her gently: 'Yes.'

She produced a packet of notepaper and envelopes, *The Monster Packet for a Penny,* all complete with a wisp of pink blotting paper and a penholder without a nib, which she had bought at the chandler's on her way home that evening, along with some sago and some hair oil for Johnny, whose stiff unruly hair provoked such spasms of rage in her bosom that she declared that she was 'sick to death of it.' On the supper table lay also a platter, a loaf, a basin of mustard pickle, and a plate with round lengths of cheese shaped like small candles.

'Devil blast him!' muttered Mrs. Flynn as she fetched from a cupboard shelf a sour-looking bottle labelled Writing Fluid, a dissolute pen, and requested Johnny to compose a letter to Stringer – devil blast him! – telling him of the plight of her daughter Pomona Flynn, about whom she desired him to know that she had already consulted her lawyers and the chief of police, and intimating that unless she heard from him satisfactory by the day after to-morrow the matter would pass out of her hands.

'That's no good, it's not the way,' declared her son thoughtfully; Mrs. Flynn therefore sat humbly confronting him and awaited the result of his cogitations. Johnny was not a very robust youth, but he was growing fast now, since he had taken up with running; he was very fleet, so Mrs. Flynn understood, and had already won a silver-plated hot-water jug, which they used for the milk. But still he was thin and not tall, his dark hair was scattered; his white face was a nice face, thought Mrs. Flynn, very nice, only there was always something strange about his clothes. She couldn't help that now, but he had such queer fancies; there was no other boy in the street whose trousers were so baggy or of such a colour. His starched collars were all right, of course, beautifully white and shiny – she got them up herself – and they set his neck off nicely.

'All we need do,' her son broke in, 'is just tell him.'

'Tell him?'

'Yes, just tell him about it – it's very unfortunate – and ask him to come and see you. I hope though,' he paused, 'I hope they won't want to go and get married.'

'He ought to be made to, devil blast him!'

cried Mrs. Flynn, 'only she's frightened, she is; afraid of her mortal life of him! We don't want him here, neither; she says he's a nasty, horrible man.'

Johnny sat dumb for some moments. Pomona was a day girl in service at a restaurant. Stringer was a clerk to an auctioneer. The figure of his pale little sister shrinking before a ruffian (whom he figured as a fat man with a red beard) startled and stung him.

'Besides,' continued Mrs. Flynn, 'he's just going to be married to some woman, some pretty judy, God help her . . . in fact, as like as not he's married to her already by now. No, I gave up that idea long ago, I did, before I told you, long ago.'

'We can only tell him about Pomony, then, and ask him what he would like to do.'

'What he would *like* to do – well, certainly!' protested the widow.

'And if he's a decent chap,' continued Johnny serenely, 'it will be all right, there won't be any difficulty. If he ain't, then we can do something else.'

His mother was reluctant to concur, but the

boy had his way. He sat with his elbows on the table, his head pressed in his hands, but he could not think out the things he wanted to say to this man. He would look up and stare around the room as if he were in a strange place, though it was not strange to him at all, for he had lived in it many years. There was not much furniture in the apartment, yet there was but little space in it. The big table was covered with American cloth, mottled and shiny. Two or three chairs, full of age and discomfort, stood upon a carpet that was full of holes and stains. There were some shelves in a recess, an engraving framed in maple of the player scene from 'Hamlet,' and near by on the wall hung a gridiron, whose prongs were woven round with coloured wools and decorated with satin bows. Mrs. Flynn had a passion for vases, and two of these florid objects, bought at a fair, companioned a clock whose once snowy face had long since turned sallow because of the oil Mrs. Flynn had administered 'to make it go properly.'

But he could by no means think out this letter; his mother sat so patiently watching him that he asked her to go and sit in the other room. Then he sat on, sniffing, as if thinking with his nose, while the room began to smell of the smoking lamp. He was remembering how, years ago, when they were little children, he had seen Pomony in her nightgown and, angered with her for some petty reason, he had punched her on the side. Pomony had turned white, she could not speak, she could not breathe. He had been momentarily proud of that blow; it was a good blow, he had never hit another boy like that. But Pomony had fallen into a chair, her face tortured with pain, her eyes filled with tears that somehow would not fall. Then a fear seized him, horrible, piercing, frantic; she was dying, she would die, and there was nothing he could do to stop her! In passionate remorse and pity, he had flung himself before her, kissing her feet – they were small and beautiful, though not very clean – until at last he had felt Pomony's arms droop caressingly around him, and heard Pomony's voice speaking lovingly and forgivingly to him.

After a decent interval his mother returned to him.

'What are we going to do about *her?*' she asked. 'She'll have to go away.'

'Away! Do you mean go to a home? No, but why go away. I'm not ashamed; what is there to be ashamed of?'

'Who the deuce is going to look after her? You talk like a tom-fool—yes, you are,' insisted Mrs. Flynn passionately. 'I'm out all day from one week's end to the other. She can't be left alone and the people downstairs are none too civil about it, as it is. She'll have to go to the workhouse, that's all.'

Johnny was aghast, indignant, and really angry. He would never, never consent to such a thing! Pomony! Into a workhouse! She should not, she should stop at home, here, like always, and have a nurse.

'Fool!' muttered his mother, with castigating scorn. 'Where's the money for nurses and doctors to come from? I've got no money for such things.'

'I'll get some!' declared Johnny hotly.

'Where?'

'I'll sell something.'

'What?'

'I'll save up.'

'How?'

'And I'll borrow some.'

'You'd better shut up now, or I'll knock your head off!' cried his mother. 'Fidding and fadding about – you're daft!'

'She shan't go to any workhouse!'

'Fool!' repeated his mother, revealing her disgust at his hopeless imbecility.

'I tell you she shall not go there!' shouted the boy, stung into angry resentment by her contempt.

'She shall, she must.'

'I say she shan't!'

'Oh, don't be such a blasted fool!' cried the distracted woman, rising from her chair.

Johnny sprang to his feet almost screaming, 'You are the blasted fool – you, you!'

Mrs. Flynn seized a table knife and struck at her son's face with it. He leaped away in terror, his startled appearance, glaring eyes, and strained figure so affecting Mrs. Flynn that she dropped the knife, and, sinking into her chair, burst into peals of hysterical laughter. Recovering himself the boy hastened to the laughing woman. The maddening peals continued and increased, shocking him, unnerving him again; she was dying,

205

she would die. His mother's laughter had always been harsh but delicious to him, it was so infectious; but this was demoniacal, it was horror.

'Oh, don't don't, mother, don't!' he cried, fondling her and pressing her yelling face to his breast. But she pushed him fiercely away, and the terrifying laughter continued to sear his very soul until he could bear it no longer. He struck at her shoulders with clenched fist, and shook her frenziedly, frantically, crying:

'Stop it, stop, oh, stop it! She'll go mad! Stop it, stop!'

He was almost exhausted, when suddenly Pomona rushed into the room in her nightgown. Her long black hair tumbled in lovely locks about her pale face and her shoulders; her feet were bare.

'Oh, Johnny, what are you doing?' gasped his little pale sister Pomony, who seemed so suddenly, so unbelievably, turned into a woman. 'Let her alone.'

She pulled the boy away, fondling and soothing their distracted mother until Mrs. Flynn partially recovered.

'Come to bed now,' commanded Pomona, and

Mrs. Flynn thereupon, still giggling, followed her child. When he was alone tremblingly Johnny turned down the lamp flame which had filled the room with smoky fumes. His glance rested upon the table knife; the room was silent and oppressive now. He glared at the picture of Hamlet, at the clock with the oily face, at the notepaper lying white upon the table. They had all turned into quivering semblances of the things they were; he was crying.

2

A letter, indited in the way he desired, was posted by Johnny on his way to work next morning. He was clerk in the warehouse of a wholesale provision merchant, and he kept tally, in some underground cellars carpeted with sawdust, of hundreds of sacks of sugar and cereals, tubs of butter, of lard, of treacle, chests of tea, a regular promontory of cheeses, cases of candles, jam, starch, and knife polish, many of them stamped with the mysterious words FACTORY BULKED. He did not like those words, they sounded ugly and their meaning was obscure.

Sometimes he took the cheese-tasting implement from the foreman's bench, and, when no one was looking, pierced it into a fine Cheddar or Stilton, withdrawing it with a little cylinder of cheese lying like a small candle in the curved blade. Then he would bite off the piece of rind, restore it neatly to the body of the cheese, and drop the other candle-like piece into his pocket. Sometimes his pocket was so full of cheese that he was reluctant to approach the foreman, fearing he would smell it. He was very fond of cheese. All of them liked cheese.

The Flynns waited several days for a reply to the letter but none came. Stringer did not seem to think it called for any reply. At the end of a week Johnny wrote again to his sister's seducer. Pomona had given up her situation at the restaurant; her brother was conspicuously and unfailingly tender to her. He saved what money he could, spent none upon himself, and brought home daily an orange or an egg for the girl. He wrote a third letter to the odious Stringer, not at all threateningly, but just invitingly, persuasively. And he waited, but waited in vain. Then in that underground cheese tunnel where he worked he began to plot an alternate course of action, and as time passed, bringing no recognition from Stringer, his plot began to crystallise and determine itself. It was nothing else than to murder the man; he would kill him, he had thought it out, it could be done. He would wait for him near Stringer's lodgings one dark night, and beat out his brains with a club. All that was necessary then would be to establish an *alibi*. For some days Johnny dwelt so gloatingly upon the details of this retribution that he forgot about the *alibi*. By this time he had accumulated from his mother – for he could never once bring himself to interrogate Pomona personally about her misfortune – sufficient description of Stringer to recognise him among a thousand, so he thought. It appeared that he was not a large man with a red beard, but a small man with glasses, spats, and a slight limp, who always attended a certain club of which he was the secretary at a certain hour on certain nights in each week. To Johnny's mind, the *alibi* was not merely important in itself, it was a romantic necessity. And it was so easy; it would be quite sufficient for Johnny to present himself at the public library, where he was fairly well-known. The library was quite close to Stringer's lodgings and they, fortunately, were in a dark, quiet little street. He would borrow a book from the odd-eyed man in the reference department, retire to one of the inner study rooms, and at half-past seven creep out unseen, creep out, creep out with his thick stick, and wait by the house in that dark, quiet little street; it was very quiet; and it would be very dark; wait there for him all in the dark, just creep quietly out – and wait. But in order to get that *alibi* quite perfect he would have to take a friend with him to the library room, so that the friend could swear that he had really been there all the time, because it was just possible the odd-eyed man wouldn't be prepared to swear to it; he did not seem able to see very much, but it was hard to tell with people like that.

Johnny Flynn had not told any of his friends about his sister's misfortune; in time, time enough, they were bound to hear of it. Of all his friends he rejected the close ones, those of whom he was very fond, and chose a stupid lump of a fellow, massive and nasal, named

Donald. Though awkward and fat, he had joined Johnny's running club; Johnny had trained him for his first race. But he had subjected Donald to such exhausting exercise, what with skipping, gymnastics, and tiring jaunts, that though his bulk disappeared his strength went with it; to Johnny's great chagrin he grew weak, and failed ignominiously in the race. Donald thereafter wisely rejected all offers of assistance and projected a training system of his own. For weeks he tramped miles into hilly country, in the heaviest of boots to which he had nailed some thick pads of lead. When he donned his light running shoes for his second race he displayed an agility and suppleness, a god-like ease, that won not only the race, but the admiration and envy of all the competitors. It was this dull, lumpish Donald that Johnny fixed upon to assist him. He was a great fool, and it would not matter if he did get himself into trouble. Even if he did, Johnny could get him out again, by confessing to the police; so that was all right. He asked Donald to go to the library with him on a certain evening to read a book called *Rasselas* – it was a grand book, very excit-

ing – and Donald said he would go. He did not
propose to tell Donald of his homicidal intention;
he would just sit him down in the library with
Rasselas, while he himself sat at another table
behind Donald, yes, behind him; even if Donald
noticed him creeping out he would say he was
only going to the counter to get another book.
It was all quite clear and safe. He would be able
to creep out, creep out, rush up to the dark little
street – yes, he would ask Donald for a piece of
that lead and wrap it round the head of the stick
– he would creep out, and in ten minutes or
twenty he would be back in the library again
asking for another book or sitting down by
Donald as if he had not been outside the place,
as if nothing had happened as far as he was
concerned, nothing at all!

The few intervening days passed with vexing
deliberation. Each night seemed the best of all
possible nights for the deed, each hour that
Stringer survived seemed a bad hour for the
world. They were bad, slow hours for Johnny,
but at last the day dawned, passed, darkness
came, and the hour rushed upon him.

He took his stick and called for Donald.

'Can't come,' said Donald, limping to the door in answer to Johnny's knock; 'I been and hurt my leg.'

For a moment Johnny was full of inward silent blasphemy that flashed from a sudden tremendous hatred, but he said calmly:

'But still . . . no, you haven't . . . what have you hurt it for?'

Donald was not able to deal with such locution. He ignored it and said:

'My knee cap, my shin. Oo, come and have a look. We was mending a flue . . . it was the old man's wheelbarrow. . . . Didn't I tell him of it neither!'

'Oh, you told him of it?'

Johnny listened to his friend's narration very abstractedly, and at last went off to the library by himself. As he walked away he was conscious of a great feeling of relief welling up in him. He could not get an *alibi* without Donald, not a sure one, so he would not be able to do anything to-night. He felt relieved, he whistled as he walked, he was happy again, but he went on to the library. He was going to rehearse the *alibi* by himself – that was the wise thing to do, of

213

course – rehearse it, practise it; it would be perfect next week when Donald was better. So he did this. He got out a book from the odd-eyed man, who strangely enough was pre-occupied and did not seem to recognise him. It was disconcerting, that; he specially wanted the man to notice him. He went into the study room rather uneasily. Ten minutes later he crept out unseen, carrying his stick – he had forgotten to ask Donald for the piece of lead – and was soon lurking in the shadow of the dark, quiet little street.

It was a perfect spot, there could not be a better place, not in the middle of a town. The house had an area entry through an iron gate; at the end of a brick pathway, over a coalplate, five or six stone steps led steeply up to a narrow front door with a brass letter box, a brass knocker, and a glazed fanlight, painted 29. The windows, too, were narrow, and the whole house had a squeezed appearance. A church clock chimed eight strokes. Johnny began to wonder what he would do, what would happen, if Stringer were suddenly to come out of that gateway. Should he – would he – could he . . .?

And then the door at the top of the steps did open wide, and framed there in the lighted space young Flynn saw the figure of his own mother.

She came down the steps alone, and he followed her short, jerky footsteps secretly until she reached the well-lit part of the town, where he joined her. It was quite simple, she explained to him with an air of superior understanding; she had just paid Mr. Stringer a visit, waiting for letters from that humbug had made her 'popped.' Had he thought she would creep on her stomach and beg for a fourpenny piece, when she could put him in jail if all were known, as she would, too, if it hadn't been for her children, poor little fatherless things? No, middling boxer, not that! So she had left off work early, had gone and caught him at his lodgings and taxed him with it. He denied of it, he was that cocky, it so mortified her that she had snatched up the clock and thrown it at him. Yes, his own clock.

'But it was only a little one, though. He was frightened out of his life and run upstairs. Then his landlady came rushing in. I told her all about it, everything, and she was that "popped" with him she give me the name and address of his fionx – their banns is been put up. She made him come downstairs and face me, and his face was as white as the driven snow, Johnny, it was. He was obliged to own up. The lady said to him, "Whatever have you been at, Mr. Stringer?" she said to him, "I can't believe it, knowing you for ten years; you must have forgot yourself." Oh, a proper understanding it was,' declared Mrs. Flynn, finally. 'His lawyers are going to write to us and put everything in order; Duckle & Hoole they are.'

Again a great feeling of relief welled up in the boy's breast, as if, having been dragged into a horrible vortex, he had been marvellously cast free again.

The days that followed were blessedly tranquil, though Johnny was often smitten with awe at the thought of what he had contemplated. That fool, Donald, too, one evening insisted on accompanying him to the library where he spent an hour of baffled understanding over the pages of *Rasselas*. But the lawyers Duckle & Hoole aroused a tumult of hatred in Mrs. Flynn. They pared down her fond anticipations to the minimum; they put so much slight upon her family, and such a gentlemanly decorum and generous forbearance upon the behaviour of their client, Mr. Stringer, that she became inarticulate. When informed that that gentleman desired no intercourse whatsoever with any Flynn, or the offspring thereof, she became speechless. Shortly, Messrs. Duckle and Hoole begged to submit for her approval a draft agreement embodying their client's terms, one provision of which was that if the said Flynns violated the agreement by taking any proceedings against the said Stringer they should thereupon, *ipso facto,* willy nilly or whatever, forfeit and pay unto him, the said Stringer, not by way of penalty but as damages, the sum of £100. Whereupon Mrs. Flynn recovered her speech and suffered a little tender irony to emerge.

The shoemaker, whose opinion upon this draft agreement was solicited, confessed himself as much baffled by its phraseology as he was idignant at its tenor and terms.

'That man,' he declared solemnly to Johnny, 'ought to have his brain knocked out;' and he

217

conveyed by subtle intimations to the boy that
that was the course he would favour were he
himself standing in Johnny's shoes. 'One dark
night,' he had roared, with a dreadful glare in
his eyes, 'with a neat heavy stick!'

The Flynns also consulted a cabman who
lodged in the house. His legal qualifications
appeared to lie in the fact that he had driven the
private coach of a major-general whose son, now
a fruit farmer in British Columbia, had once
been entered for the Bar. The cabman was a
very positive and informative cabman. 'List and
learn,' he would say, 'list and learn'; and he
would regale Johnny, or anyone else, with an
oration to which you might listen as hard as
you liked but from which you could not learn.
He was husky, with a thick red neck and the
cheek bones of a horse. Having perused the
agreement with one eye judiciously cocked, the
other being screened by a drooping lid adorned
with a glowing nodule, he carefully refolded
the folios and returned them to the boy.

'Any judge – who was up to snuff – would
impound that dockyment.'

'What's that?'

'They would impound it,' repeated the cabman, smiling wryly.

'But what's "impound it"? What for?'

'I tell you it would be impounded that dockyment would,' asseverated the cabman. Once more he took the papers from Johnny, opened them out, reflected upon them and returned them again without a word. Catechism notwithstanding, the oracle remained impregnable, mystifying.

The boy continued to save his pocket money. His mother went about her work with a grim air, having returned the draft agreement to the lawyers with an ungracious acceptance of terms.

One April evening Johnny went home to an empty room. Pomona was out. He prepared his tea, and afterwards sat reading *Tales of a Grandfather*. That was a book if anybody wanted a book! When darkness came he descended the stairs to enquire of the shoemaker's wife about Pomony; he was anxious. The shoemaker's wife was absent, too, and it was late when she returned, accompanied by his mother.

Pomona's hour had come. They had taken

her to the workhouse – only just in time – a little
boy – they were both all right – he was an uncle!

His mother's deceit stupefied him; he felt
ashamed, deeply shamed; but after a while that
same recognisable feeling of relief welled up in
his breast and drenched him with satisfactions.
After all, what could it matter where a person
was born, or where one died, as long as you had
your chance of growing up at all, and, if lucky,
of growing up all right? But this babe, had got to
bear the whole burden of its father's misdeed,
though; it had got to behave itself or it would
have to pay its father a hundred pounds as
damages. Perhaps that was what that queer bit
of poetry meant, 'The child is father of the man.'

His mother swore that they were very good
and clean and kind at the workhouse, everything of the best and most expensive; there was
nothing she would have liked better than to
have gone there herself when Johnny and
Pomony were born.

'And if ever I have any more,' Mrs. Flynn
sighed, but with profound conviction, 'I will
certainly go there.'

Johnny gave her half the packet of peppermints he had bought for Pomona. With some of his saved money he bought her a bottle of stout – she looked tired and sad – she was very fond of stout. The rest of the money he gave her for to buy Pomony something when she visited her. He would not go himself to visit her, not there. He spent the long intervening evenings at the library – the odd-eyed man had shown him a lovely book about birds. He was studying it. On Sundays, in the spring, he was going out to catch birds himself, out in the country, with a catapult. The cuckoo was a marvellous bird. So was a titlark. Donald Gower found a goatsucker's nest last year.

Then one day he ran from work all the way home, knowing Pomony would at last be there. He walked slowly up the street to recover his breath. He stepped up the stairs, humming quite casually, and tapped at the door of their room – he did not know why he tapped. He heard Pomony's voice calling him. A thinner, paler Pomony stood by the hearth, nursing a white-clothed bundle, the fat pink babe.

'Oh, my dear!' cried her ecstatic brother, 'the beauty he is! What larks we'll have with him!'

He took Pomona into his arms, crushing the infant against her breast and his own. But she did not mind. She did not rebuke him, she even let him dandle her precious babe.

'Look, what is his name to be, Pomony? Let's call him Rasselas.'

Pomona looked at him very doubtfully.

'Or would you like William Wallace, then, or Robert Bruce?'

'I shall call him Johnny,' said Pomona.

'Oh, that's silly!' protested her brother. But Pomona was quite positive about this. He fancied there were tears in her eyes, she was always tender-hearted.

'I shall call him Johnny – Johnny Flynn.'

A LIST OF VOLUMES ISSUED IN THE TRAVELLERS' LIBRARY

JONATHAN CAPE LTD.
THIRTY BEDFORD SQUARE LONDON

THE TRAVELLERS' LIBRARY

★

A series of copyright books in all branches of litera
designed primarily for the pocket or kit-bag, but als(
the small house where shelf space is scarce and where
small books are more welcome than one large one.

Though the volumes measure only 7 inches by 4¾ in(
the page is arranged so that the margins are not unrea
ably curtailed nor legibility sacrificed.   The books a
a uniform thickness irrespective of the number of p
and the paper, which is specially manufactured for
series, is remarkably opaque, even when it is thinnest.

A semi-flexible form of binding has been adopted, as a
guard against the damage inevitably associated with h
packing.   The cloth is made specially for the purpose
particularly attractive shade of blue and has the autl
name stamped in gold on the back.

Each volume costs 5s. net

★

1. CAN SUCH THINGS BE?   A volume of Storie
      by Ambrose Bierce

¶ 'Bierce never wastes a word, never coins a too startling ph
   he secures his final effect, a cold thrill of fear, by a simple
   subtle, realism.   No anthology of short stories, limited to a
   or so, would be complete without an example of his ur
                         artistry.'   *Morning Post*

2. THE BLACK DOG   A volume of Stories
      by A. E. Coppard

¶ 'Mr. Coppard is a born story-teller.   The book is filled
   a variety of delightful stuff: no one who is interested in
   writing in general, and good short stories in particular, sh
                         miss it.'   *Spectator*

THE AUTOBIOGRAPHY of a SUPER-TRAMP
by W. H. Davies. With a preface by G. Bernard Shaw

Printed as it was written, it is worth reading for its literary style alone. The author tells us with inimitable quiet modesty of how he begged and stole his way across America and through England and Wales until his travelling days were cut short by losing his right foot while attempting to 'jump' a train.

BABBITT   A Novel
by Sinclair Lewis

One of the greatest novels I have read for a long time.' *H. G. Wells*   'Babbitt is a triumph.'   *Hugh Walpole*
His work has that something extra, over and above, which makes the work of art, and it is signed in every line with the unique personality of the author.'   *Rebecca West*

THE CRAFT OF FICTION
by Percy Lubbock

No more substantial or more charming volume of criticism has been published in our time.'   *Observer*
To say that this is the best book on the subject is probably true; but it is more to the point to say that it is the only one.'
Times Literary Supplement

EARLHAM
by Percy Lubbock

The book seems too intimate to be reviewed. We want to be allowed to read it, and to dream over it, and keep silence about it. His judgment is perfect, his humour is true and ready; his touch light and prim; his prose is exact and clean and full of music.'   *Times*

WIDE SEAS & MANY LANDS A Personal Narrative
by Arthur Mason. With an Introduction by
MAURICE BARING

This is an extremely entertaining, and at the same time, moving book. We are in the presence of a born writer. We read with the same mixture of amazement and delight that fills us throughout a Conrad novel.'   *New Statesman*

8. SELECTED PREJUDICES   A book of Essays
by H. L. Mencken

¶ 'He is exactly the kind of man we are needing, an iconoc
a scoffer at ideals, a critic with whips and scorpions who
not hesitate to deal with literary, social and political hum'
in the one slashing fashion.' *English Review*

9. THE MIND IN THE MAKING   An Essay
by James Harvey Robinson

¶ 'For me, I think James Harvey Robinson is going to be al»
as important as was Huxley in my adolescence, and William J.
in later years. It is a cardinal book. I question whether in
long run people may not come to it, as making a new initia
into the world's thought and methods.' *From the Introducti»*

H. G. WELLS

10. THE WAY OF ALL FLESH   A Novel
by Samuel Butler

¶ 'It drives one almost to despair of English Literature when
sees so extraordinary a study of English life as Butler's posthur
Way of All Flesh making so little impression. Really, the En,
do not deserve to have great men.' *George Bernard Sha»*

11. EREWHON   A Satire
by Samuel Butler

¶ 'To lash the age, to ridicule vain pretension, to expose hypoc
to deride humbug in education, politics and religion, are
beyond most men's powers ; but occasionally, very occasion
a bit of genuine satire secures for itself more than a passing
of recognition. *Erewhon*, I think, is such a satire. . . .
best of its kind since *Gulliver's Travels*.' *Augustine Birre*

12. EREWHON REVISITED   A Satire
by Samuel Butler

¶ 'He waged a sleepless war with the mental torpor of the p
perous, complacent England around him, and he brought
the field a rarely paralleled versitality of talent and resource
Swift with the soul of music in him, and completely sane
liberator of humanity operating with the wit and malice
coolness of Mephistopheles.' *Manchester Guardian*

ADAM AND EVE AND PINCH ME Stories
by A. E. Coppard

Mr. Coppard's implicit theme is the closeness of the spiritual world to the material; the duality of every human nature; the strange, communicative sympathy which strikes through two temperaments and suddenly makes them one. He deals with those sudden impulses under which secrecy is broken down for a moment, the cloud-veil of convention riven, and personality revealed as under a flash of spiritual lightning.

DUBLINERS A volume of Stories
by James Joyce

A collection of fifteen short stories by the author of *Ulysses*. They are all of them brave, relentless, and sympathetic pictures of Dublin life; realistic, perhaps, but not crude; analytical, but not repugnant. No modern writer has greater significance than Mr. Joyce, whose conception and practise of the short story is certainly unique and certainly vital.

DOG AND DUCK
by Arthur Machen

'As a literary artist, Mr. Arthur Machen has few living equals, and that is very far indeed from being his only, or even his greatest, claim on the suffrages of English readers.' *Sunday Times*

KAI LUNG'S GOLDEN HOURS
by Ernest Bramah

'It is worthy of its forerunner. There is the same plan, exactitude, working-out and achievement; and therefore complete satisfaction in the reading.' *From the Preface by* HILAIRE BELLOC

ANGELS & MINISTERS, AND OTHER PLAYS
by Laurence Housman

Imaginary portraits of political characters done in dialogue— Queen Victoria, Disraeli, Gladstone, Parnell, Joseph Chamberlain, and Woodrow Wilson.

'It is all so good that one is tempted to congratulate Mr. Housman on a true masterpiece.' *Times*

18. THE WALLET OF KAI LUNG
by Ernest Bramah

¶ 'Something worth doing and done. . . . It was a thing inten[.] wrought out, completed and established. Therefore it destined to endure, and, what is more important, it w[.] success.' *Hilaire Belloc*

19. TWILIGHT IN ITALY
by D. H. Lawrence

¶ This volume of travel vignettes in North Italy was first publi[.] in 1916. Since then Mr. Lawrence has increased the num[.] of his admirers year by year. In *Twilight in Italy* they will all the freshness and vigour of outlook which they have com[.] expect from its author.

20. THE DREAM   A Novel
by H. G. Wells

¶ 'It is the richest, most generous and absorbing thing that Wells has given us for years and years.' *Daily News*
'I find this book as close to being magnificent as any book I have ever read.   It is full of inspiration and life.' *Daily Graphic*

21. ROMAN PICTURES
by Percy Lubbock

¶ Pictures of life as it is lived—or has been or might be live[.] among the pilgrims and colonists in Rome of more or English speech.
'A book of whimsical originality and exquisite workmans[.] and worthy of one of the best prose writers of our time.' *Sunday Times*

22. CLORINDA WALKS IN HEAVEN
by A. E. Coppard

¶ 'Genius is a hard-ridden word, and has been put by critic[.] many puny ditches, but Mr. Coppard sets up a fence worth[.] its mettle.   He shows that in hands like his the English lang[.] is as alive as ever, and that there are still infinite possibilitie[.] the short story.' *Outlook*

LONDON
JONATHAN CAPE THIRTY BEDFORD SQUARE